SEDUCING HER FATHER'S

ENEMY
BY
STACY-DEANNE

Readers: Thanks so much for choosing my book! I would be very appreciative if you would leave reviews when you are done. Much love!

Email: stacydeanne1@aol.com

Website: Stacy's Website [1]

Facebook: Stacy's Facebook Profile[2]

Twitter: Stacy's Twitter[3]

Other titles by Stacy-Deanne Include:

Bruised Series

Stripped Series

Tate Valley Sexy Suspense Series

Seven's Deadly Sins

Prey

The Princess and the Thief

The Little Girl

The Stranger

Oleander

TO RECEIVE BOOK ANNOUNCEMENTS subscribe to Stacy's mailing list: Mailing List[4]

---

1.   https://www.stacy-deanne.com/

2.   https://www.facebook.com/stacy.deanne.5

3.   https://twitter.com/stacydeanne

4. http://eepurl.com/dFGzTL

Want recommendations on great BWWM books and authors? Stop by BWWM Romance Books on Facebook and find some great reads!

BWWM Romance Books[5]

CHAPTER ONE

"**H**elp!" Diana Wayans shoved the Goliath brute off her and raced up the carpeted stairs.

"Come back here, bitch."

With her heart beating in her throat and eyes cloudy from tears, Diana ran toward her bedroom, but the man snatched her from behind before she could enter.

"No!" She swung her arms, kicking. "Someone, help me! Help!"

"Shut up." He carried her into the room and pushed her against the wall. "Mm. Look at those pretty...ass...eyes. You want to lose one of 'em?" He pulled a lighter from his black hoodie and raised it to her face. "This is the last time I'll ask you." He snatched her neck. "Where is George?"

"Please." Diana shivered, digging her fingers into the wall. "I don't know where my father is. I swear."

He moved the lighter closer to her eye, teasing the button with his thumb. "You're lying."

"I'm telling the truth." Diana studied his menacing eyes, trying to pinpoint his next move.

He stroked her shoulder-length, brownish-black crinkles. "You're gonna tell me where that nigger is or I'll barbecue your eye." He pushed the button and a tiny flame danced from the lighter.

"Okay." She took a deep breath. "He called me and told me to leave Atlanta."

The man's fat lips formed a smirk, the stench of peppers and sausage shooting through his breath.

"He didn't say why. He just told me to leave because I was in danger."

He lowered the lighter to her stacked bosom. "Do you know who I work for?"

She shook her head.

"I work for Milan Vitale."

Diana swallowed. "The mobster?"

He nodded.

"How in hell did my father get mixed up with him?"

"George is priority number one on our list." He ran his finger across her honey-brown cheek. "Your father spent his life fucking over people but he won't get away with double-crossing Milan." His fluffy eyebrows rose. "I wish you and me had met under better circumstances. Who'd have known George's daughter was such a beautiful woman?" He glanced at the queen-sized bed covered in lavender sheets. "I want your last moment to be enjoyable."

"You won't get away with this." Diana straightened her 5'9 stature. "My ex is a cop and he'll search every inch of this earth for you if you hurt me."

He leaned into her, winking. "I'll take that chance." As he grabbed her waist, she stomped on his foot, slugged him, and ran to the nightstand.

"Come here!" He yanked her hair, flung her around and punched her.

The pain echoed through her teeth while salty, bitter blood trickled inside her mouth.

"You got moves, huh?" He gave her an obnoxious kiss, licking her blood from his lips afterwards. "I didn't expect that."

She head-butted him and when he fell back, Diana got her gun from inside the nightstand. "Don't move!"

"Oh, what you got there, hmm?" His eyes flashed with wickedness. "A little gun?" He cackled, slipping his own from his back pocket. "This is the game you wanna play? I bet I'm a better shooter than you." He licked his lips. "Is that gun even real?"

"Don't make me do this." Her voice shook. "Just leave me alone."

"Your father screwed my boss over and if he doesn't pay, you will."

She inched back as he approached, gun trembling in her hand. "Don't come near me."

"This isn't you, Diana." He continued toward her. "You're not a killer. You're a good woman. A sensual woman."

"Stop!" She held her wrist to steady the wobbling gun. "I swear I'll shoot you."

"You know what I think?" He aimed his gun at her. "You're just as much of a liar as your father."

Diana shot, the force jolting her from where she stood.

"Ah." The man gasped and gurgled as he fell to the floor, his chest oozing with blood.

AFTER BEING QUESTIONED several times by her ex-boyfriend Eric Sachs and having her bedroom examined, Diana watched from her living room window as the last two officers drove away.

"Now what?" She rested her face against the curtains. "Do I have anything to worry about?"

Eric read his tiny notepad. "It was self-defense."

She turned from the window, griping the curtain's pleaded fabric. "How can you be sure?"

He slipped the notepad into his back pocket, his shoulder holster jiggling. "Trust me. This is clean cut."

"But people go to prison all the time for self-defense."

The silver sparks in his blue eyes resembled the icy mountains of Antarctica. "You're a registered gun owner, he broke into your home and tried to kill you. You have nothing to worry about."

She broke from the paradise his enchanting eyes provided. "Except a member of the Mafia just tried to kill me, I guess."

He sighed, his dimples protruding from his oval cheeks. "Sure you don't need to go to the hospital?" He touched her swollen jaw. "He landed a good punch. I'm glad the asshole's dead."

"I'm okay." She moved away from him though a part of her wanted to sink into his caring embrace. "All on my mind is finding out what the hell my father's gotten into."

"What's the deal?" Eric scratched underneath his golden bangs. "You seemed weird when I ran into you the other day. Like something was bothering you."

"It's not your problem."

"It used to be." He stroked the blond fuzz on his chin. "Just because we're not together anymore doesn't mean I just stop caring. I'll always care about you, Di. Now what's going on?"

"George called me a few nights ago."

"Your father? What the hell did he want?"

"He wanted me to leave because I was in danger." She slapped her thighs as she sat on the wooden coffee table. "He wouldn't say why and though he tried to hide it, I could hear the fear in his voice. I can't remember my father ever being scared."

"You barely remember your *father*." He sat beside her.

"Eric."

"Well, he abandoned you and your mom when you were a kid and sorry but this dipping in and out of your life whenever he feels like it doesn't qualify as quality time in my book."

"Milan Vitale is after him."

"The head of the Southern Italian Mafia? Why?"

"Could be any reason." She scratched through her hair. "My dad's always been reckless and irresponsible with no regard for his own life let alone others. No telling what he's done."

"Why can't he just stay gone? Every time he shows up he turns your life upside down. How long you gonna put up with it? Why can't you close the door on him forever?"

"Because he's my father."

"You're thirty-four, Di. He wasn't here for you when you were a kid, you don't need his ass now."

"No matter what, he's still blood. Just because he abandoned me doesn't mean I'll do the same."

"You always gotta be the martyr?" Eric squeezed his knees. "Shit, Di your father is why we broke up."

"What in the world does he have to do with us?"

"Because he was never around when you needed him, you don't trust men. That's why you couldn't commit."

"I didn't commit?" She chuckled, pointing at herself. "As I remember it, I did everything for you, Eric. You were my world."

"All I wanted was to make you happy." He pressed his thin lips together. "But, you wouldn't let me. Always had to be in control of everything."

"I don't have to listen to this." She stood and turned her back to him.

"That's the only way you're comfortable isn't it, Di? If you aren't pulling the strings then you're too afraid to take a chance."

"I was almost killed today, Eric." She faced him. "Yet you can turn this around to be about you as usual."

"It's about *us*, Di." He rose with sad, puppy dog eyes. "We should be ashamed of ourselves for turning our backs on what we had. I love you."

She closed her eyes.

"We belong together. I don't care how you rationalize why we shouldn't be together, it won't change how much I love you."

"There are more important things going on than you and me."

He held his waist, the dynamic creases in his face curving into a frown.

"What's important is this mess my dad's got going with Milan. As much as I resent George, I can't let anything happen to him."

"What the hell can you do?"

She shrugged. "I got to find out where my dad is before Milan does."

Eric scratched the back of his faded haircut. "Good luck with that. The Navy Seals couldn't find your dad. No one and I mean *no* one can find George Wayans unless he wants to be found. You'd have a better shot finding Big Foot."

"I can't just do nothing."

His spicy cologne tickled her nose.

"I need your help."

"How the hell can a country-ass cop from Atlanta help you with a person as powerful as Milan Vitale?"

"You have friends who can help." She touched his plaid shirt, his rolled up sleeves showing off his fit forearms. "Davis Miller comes to mind. You said he owes you a favor."

He moved away from her. "Jeez, Di."

"Who better to ask for help than an FBI agent who works organized crime? If anyone knows the secrets of the Vitale Organization, it's Davis."

"And you think he can just tell us stuff? Whatever he does, it's classified."

"I need answers." She grabbed his hand. "I need you to talk to him for me or give me his information."

He exhaled, pinching the bridge of his nose. "Can't believe I'm doing this."

"You said you'd do anything for me."

He grimaced. "Looks like I'm living to regret it."

CHAPTER TWO

S everal days later, Diana plopped on her couch and dropped her head after hearing Eric's disappointing news. "Davis knows nothing?"

Eric rocked with his hands in his pockets. "Not concerning your father and Milan, no."

"Shit."

"He says agents have been working inside the Vitale Empire for years and could be close to nailing Milan, but Davis isn't holding his breath."

Diana sunk into the pillows. "Why not?"

"The feds have had leaks into the Vitale business since Milan's father ran it."

"Didn't his father die?"

"Last year." He sat with her. "Luca had been ailing for years with dementia. That's why he retired from the business. Anyway, Davis didn't know anything that would help you. Sorry."

She laid her head on his wide shoulder. "Thanks for trying."

"Davis might not have come up with anything but I did. Ever heard of a man named Gray Malton?"

She scrunched up her mouth. "Should I have?"

"He's a big time art dealer who works with celebrities, politicians, anyone who is anyone."

"So?"

"I was Googling Milan and found out he gets his pieces through Malton."

Diana rose from the pillows. "Art, huh?"

He took out his phone and showed her a picture of a peachy-white man with uneven skin and a fabricated smile as if he tried to convey confidence but had none.

"Is this Malton?"
Eric nodded.
Gray dressed as if he were drowning in money but his awkward pose showed a man always chasing after what he couldn't have.
Eric took the phone and pulled up another picture. "Davis sent me this."
Diana looked at the picture of a clean-cut man whose skin glowed like alabaster silk with a natural golden hue.
His grand suit didn't hide his athletic build or those strong shoulders that forced your attention even more than his exquisite, shadowy eyes.
"Who..." Diana cleared her throat. "Who is this?"
"That's the man himself."
"This is Milan Vitale?"
He wore his raven hair low on the sides almost as short as Eric's with the top swept back into chic waves.
"How can this be Milan?" She shivered, fearing if she looked into his eyes too long she'd drown in them. "He looks our age."
"He's thirty-seven."
The words caught in her throat. "I didn't realize he was so young."
"Good-looking too?" Jealousy seeped from Eric's tone. "Don't let the baby face and come-hither eyes fool you. He's the most dangerous man you'll ever come across."

Diana swallowed, staring at the way Milan's scruffy beard caressed his oblong cheeks. "It's weird now that I can put a name to the face. He looks so normal. Not like the monster you hear about." She passed Eric his phone, still staring at Milan's face. "Tell me more about this Malton."

"Milan gets all of his art from Gray and he's a big art lover. Apparently their friends or whatever. Davis says Malton's having some annual charity event on his yacht next weekend where he'll be donating the proceeds from his guests to breast cancer."

She snickered. "Interesting."

"I don't like that look in your eyes, Di."

"Malton deals art and art's my specialty. We'd be a match made in heaven."

"You're a graphic designer and he's an art buyer. Not exactly the same thing."

"But I know art." She bit her lip. "This will give me an in."

"What are you talking about?"

"Going to Miami and doing anything I can to find out why Milan wants my father dead."

Eric glared at her, brow furrowing. "What the hell did you say?"

"You heard me. I'll use my charm and wit to find out what's going on."

"Are you insane?" Eric jumped up. "No way in hell am I letting you do this. It's too dangerous."

She rose. "And I told you I don't have a choice."

"Think, woman." He tapped her forehead. "Milan sent a man to your home to kill you. Now you wanna go meet him? How in your mind does that make sense?"

"He won't know it's me." She got her bottled water from the table and sipped. "I'm going undercover."

"Undercover?" His face turned red as he half-chuckled. "You're not a damn cop."

"That thug said it surprised him that I was so beautiful which means Milan doesn't know what I look like. How could they? I don't even use pics on my social media, just of graphics from my portfolio."

"No." Eric rubbed his brow. "No."

"I don't think talking to Gray Malton is so dangerous. If I appeal to him with the common interest of art then—"

"No!"

"He can get me close to Milan and that's what I need." She touched his arm. "Eric, you taught me how to protect myself and be careful. I have a gun, remember?"

"Milan will kill you without thinking twice if he found out who you were. You're not equipped for this. We can go to the Miami Police. Let them handle it."

"Like they will take this seriously and what can they do against Milan if the FBI can't even get him? I don't care about his organization or what he does, I only care about his connection to my father."

Eric leaned back, clasping his head with both hands. "Is there anything I can do to stop you?"

"No."

"Fuck." He dropped his arms. "Then I'm going with you."

"I can't let you do that."

"There's no way in hell I'm letting you put your life in danger alone. Besides I'm the cop, not you. I need to be there to make sure you're okay."

She tucked in her lips, overtaken by his sincerity. "Thank you so much."

"We do this but we do it my way, Diana." He pointed to her. "We'll need fake identities and we need to be damn convincing because Milan's people will do background checks before anyone gets near him. You'll swear the freaking government was on your ass when he gets through with us."

"As long as everything checks out we'll be all right."

"Davis can start a paper trail for us and invent our pasts so it looks like we are who we say we are. We're gonna need fake social security numbers, fake birth certificates, licenses, anything to make our new identities look real."

"Okay." Diana nodded, heart pounding from adrenaline.

"I'd be fired from the department if they found out I was helping a civilian infiltrate the Mob."

"Yeah, what about the department? How will you get away?"
"I'll tell the chief I got personal business to handle."

"I don't want you to lie."

"I have no choice, but if they find out about this my career with the Atlanta PD is over."

"You sure you want to do this?" She drew closer to him. "Sacrifice your career for me? Being a cop means so much to you."
The lines around his mouth relaxed as he caressed her cheek. "Nothing means more to me than you."

CHAPTER THREE

Miami, Florida (Milan Vitale's Estate)

"Douglas?" Milan's butler entered the den. "Mr. Vitale will see you now."

"It's about time." At 6'5, the burly black man fastened his Gucci blazer and followed the butler to Milan's steam room.

Milan sauntered out the foggy room with a white towel hugging his masculine waist and sweat sprinkling his firm pecs. "Leave us," he ordered the butler, and the man left. "Hello, Douglas. How are you today?"

Douglas shook his long dreads out his face. "Fine."

"You sure?" Milan walked toward him in flip-flops. "I sense something bothering you."

"Just a little tense." Douglas clasped his hands in front of him. "Nothing to worry about."

"You need a beautiful woman to help you relax." Milan sipped from his water bottle. "Borrow one from my collection. I can't entertain all of them."

"I got more important things to think about than women."

"Doesn't seem like that with Pam."

Douglas straightened his posture.

"Take someone else and get Pam out your system."

"I like Pam in my system." He looked at his fingernails. "Besides, you haven't been with a woman in a while either. Why don't you use that collection for yourself?"

Milan sat on the suede bench. "I'm tired of dabbling in art I don't plan to buy."

"So you're looking for love?"

He shrugged a shoulder as he drank. "This is about your well-being. You're my right-hand man so I gotta do all I can to keep you on your game. If that means getting you pussy, that's what I'll do."

"Thought Ramon was your number one. I mean, he'll move the earth for you, wouldn't he?"

"I never understood why you two can't get along."

"He's a snake, and I told you to watch your back."

"Those are some strong accusations you're throwing against your brother."

"We're not brothers."

"Oh, yes you are. We're all brothers, Douglas." Milan's eyelids pulsated. "When you're a part of the organization, you're family and don't forget it. I wish you two could stop this bickering and get along. It's starting to impact getting your jobs done."

"Ramon can't be trusted. You'll learn that one day."

"You still think Ramon is the leak?"

Douglas squinted. "How do you know he's not?"

"Because I've known Ramon since we were eighteen. He's always had my back and would die for me."

"He's just waiting." Douglas rocked his head. "Waiting to get you out the way so he can take over. What the hell was your father thinking making him a beneficiary to the empire?"

"Enough." Milan swallowed, his neck wrinkling. "I need you to keep your eyes and ears open and find out who the leak really is. As for Ramon, you will not speak about him in this manner to me again. Do you hear me?"

"Yes."

"There are more important things you need to worry about besides Ramon. Ernesto is still missing."

"He never came back from Atlanta?"

"No." Milan massaged his knuckles, staring into space. "Last time I heard from him was when he called to tell me he'd made it to Diana Wayans' home. I haven't heard from him since."

"Did he take care of Diana?"

"Forget the bitch. We need to find *George*."

"Hmm." Douglas rocked on his heels. "Isn't that Ramon's job or has he been too busy hitting on Pam?"

"Find him, Douglas." Milan glared at him. "I can't let George get away with what he's done."

A WEEK LATER

"Okay here's another joke!" Gray Malton stood in the cocktail lounge of his yacht, waving his martini. "If you don't laugh at this one, then you have no sense of humor whatsoever." He told another joke that lead to mumbles and groans from his posh guests.

"Jesus, he's such a dork." Diana sat at the bar in a silver sequined dress that cost less than a hundred dollars but went toe-to-toe with the Isaac Mizrahi gowns in the room. "Men like Gray prove that money doesn't guarantee style or class."

"The more he drinks the worse the jokes get." Eric bit into his third stuffed mushroom, and Diana struggled to ignore how scrumptious he looked in his tux.

He chewed and swallowed, staring at her.

"What?" She sucked the bitter aftertaste of vodka tonic from her lips. "Why are you staring at me like you've been hit by a truck?"

"I've never seen you like this before." His gaze fell to her bosom. "You've always been gorgeous, but you clean up well Miss Diana."

She smirked. "So I don't stick out like a sore thumb?"

"Hell no." Eric glanced around, his face glowing from the sparkle of evening gowns and chandelier lights. "You're the most beautiful woman in here. If I just met you, I'd think you were born into this life."

Gray mingled in the crowd clinking glasses with men and women who could buy Miami with the snap of their fingers.

"This yacht is bigger than my neighborhood," Diana mumbled. "Money dripping from the walls. I wonder if any of them appreciate it. I bet they spend every moment trying to get more."

"Money and power." Eric propped his elbow on the granite bar top, facing away from the bartenders. "You got that and you own the world, Di."

"Cops should be rich."

He squinted.

"Eric, you risk your life every day to keep people safe and you have to fight the city for every penny. While these people..."

A group of men swept past, leaving stinky cologne in their wake.

"Just wake up in the mornings and get everything they want. They don't have to work for it."

"They work. Just their work's different."

Diana patted the pearl clip holding her French roll in place. "They didn't work *enough*."

"Admit it." He winked. "You've wondered what it's like to be rich. This is the only shot we'll get to sample the good life."

"Is that what you want?" She set her glass on the counter. "The good life? I never pegged you for buying into this stuff."

"Nothing wrong with having money."

"Hmm." Her silver, drape earrings tickled her shoulders when she moved her head. "Guess you learn something new about a person every day."

"Yep, I wouldn't mind being rich and living like this, Di." He straightened his spine and made eye contact. "But, I'd trade it all for love."

CHAPTER FOUR

Gray escaped the men who spoke about the Miami Dolphins and their offshore accounts and went back to what he'd been doing since the party began; watching the hypnotic black woman at the bar.

She crossed her long, creamy legs and the slit of her dress opened, revealing her thigh. Her skin seemed so smooth it would be hard to grip but he'd try. She commanded his attention without even batting an eye.

Remembering this was his party, his yacht, and he was the master of the evening, he strolled toward the woman and grabbed her hand. "Hello."

She batted her sweeping lashes, those blazing hazel eyes wrapping their arms around his soul. "Uh, hello."

He kissed her hand, inhaling her mandarin perfume. "I'm Gray Malton and it's lovely to meet you." He'd intended to say something smoother but Milan had always warned him about trying too hard.

"I know who you are." She smiled, but it seemed to be subdued. "This is your party. It's nice to meet you, Mr. Malton."

"Gray, please." He sat at the bar determined not to let go of her hand for nothing in the world. "I have to be honest."

She parted her valentine lips, wetness glistening in the corners.

"I don't care if this sounds corny, but I can't take my eyes off you." She giggled. "That's sweet."

He circled his thumb over her hand. "I hope I'm not coming on too strong."

"No." She took her hand back to his dismay. "I'm Anna Hampton." She crossed her legs tighter, holding the slit. "I'm here on vacation."

"*Anna.*" The name swirled inside his head. "Where are you from? How long will you be in town?"

"I'm from Los Angeles. Not sure how long I'll be in town."

"Born in Los Angeles? I hear a little Southern accent there."

"My family's from the south." She cleared her throat. "Miami is beautiful."

"Yes." He stared into her succulent cleavage. "It sure is. How did you come to hear about this party?"

"I made it my mission to find out everything about Gray Malton." She winked. "I came to Miami for *you.*"

His testicles throbbed. "Me?"

"I want to speak to you about art." She wiggled her sharp nose. "I'm interested in doing business with you."

He cleared his throat, the head of his penis widening. "Um, you're too kind, Anna. But there are many good art dealers in LA. Why would you come all the way to Miami just to talk to me?"

"You're a major mover of landscape art and that's what I collect." She ran her finger around the rim of her glass, looking at him through her lashes. "You have an inside to the best up-and-coming artists and I want to snatch their work before they get too famous."

He crossed his legs before his dick hopped out his pants. "I'm impressed."

"You're familiar with artists that do customized portraits for clients. Is that true?"

"Yes." His face got hot. "You want to buy for your personal collection?"

"Yes just for me." She stuck out her shapely bosom. "I'd like to look at options."

"Ever worked with a dealer before?"

"Not one with your expertize, no. I'm sure I can't afford you but it never hurts to try right?"

"No." His nipples hardened as he patted her knee. "I'm sure I can get you something you love."

She shivered when he touched her.

"Oh." He moved his hand. "I'm sorry. I didn't mean to make you uncomfortable."

"No." She smiled, but he sensed how uncomfortable it made her. "It's fine."

Shit. Milan told me about going in too fast too soon.

"May I ask you a personal question?" he asked. "That guy you were with, is he your lover?"

"No." She broke eye contact, signaling there was more to the story.

"You're not together? Hard to believe. Something must be wrong with him."

"Men and women can be friends, Gray."

"A man can't be just friends with *you*, Anna. That's not possible."

She blushed. "Stop."

"It's your fault." He smiled. "You're controlling me right now. I'm thinking out loud."

"Come on, now." She tapped his leg, chuckling. "You'll be able to keep your mind on business, won't you?"

"There's one thing you should know about me, Anna." He clamped his bottom lip between his teeth. "I never make promises I can't keep. I'd love to show you around Miami while you're here. Why don't we have lunch tomorrow at my place? I can show you some art and we can talk more about what you're looking for."

"Um—"

"I'll be a gentleman, and I have plenty of servants to hear if you scream." He laughed.

"Cute."

"Where are you staying?"

"The Park City Hotel."

"Oh, lovely isn't it?" He took out his cell phone. "Beautiful view of the beach and ocean from the hotel, huh?"

"Yes, it is."

"May I have your number?"

She told him and he put it in his phone.

"Great." He passed her his card. "My personal and business numbers are on there. We'll have lunch tomorrow."

She lifted her glass and smiled.

CHAPTER FIVE

"Hello."

Eric turned from watching the fabulous ocean view on the deck of the yacht.

Behind him stood an elegant, tall woman with a platinum-blonde pixie haircut and Bette Davis eyes. The skirt of her sheer, emerald-green dress blew around her bountiful hips and settled over her chiseled legs.

"You look like a fish out of water," she said.

Eric did a double-take. Diana owned his heart but this woman was one of the sexiest he'd ever seen. "I'm sorry?"

She leaned over the yacht, diamonds dripping from her rosy-white wrists and neck. "You don't belong. Don't take it as an insult. I don't belong here either."

He whistled, giving her the once-over. "I'd beg to differ."

The tiny mole beside her nostril wasn't noticeable until she grinned. "Don't let the diamonds and the fancy dress fool you. Are you a cop?"

Shit. Is it that obvious?

"Why would you say that?"

"Because you have that same suspicious glare all cops have." She wrapped her provocative lips over the rim of her champagne glass and sipped. "I've been watching you and you analyze everything."

He gripped the railing, his watch peeking from his sleeve. "Like you've been analyzing me?"

She smirked, her chandelier earrings blowing in the breeze.

"You've known a lot of cops?"

"A few. Am I right about you?"

"Forget *me*." He crossed his arms wondering if she had any connection to Milan. "I'm more interested in knowing who *you* are."

"Nah, you're the talk of the party." She smoothed her hand over her haircut. It was perfect for her delicate face. "People have been wondering about you and your friend because no one knows you. You're not in Gray's circle."

He leaned into her to ramp up the charm though something about her told him she wouldn't be easy to manipulate. "I still wanna know your name."

She held out her hand. "I'm Pamela Peacock. You are?"

He kissed her hand. "Eric Carter. My friend and I are visiting from LA. She's here to see Gray about buying some art."

She looked at him with half-moon eyes. "Uh-huh."

"It's the truth." He chuckled. "You're a friend of Gray's?"

"No." The tight bodice held her plump, blushing breasts in place. "This charity is important to me. The proceeds from the party go to breast cancer research and I had a scare a year back."

"Glad it was just a scare."

"I'm a singer."

He glanced at the bright red tattoo of a heart pierced with a golden arrow on her shoulder.

"I sing at the Strawberry Lounge."

Milan's club. Bingo.

"I've heard of it," Eric said. "What kind of music do you sing?"

"Slow songs, jazz, R&B and soul."

"Are you a good singer?"

"I'm great." She took a card from her sequined purse and handed it to him. "Go to my website. It lists the times for my shows if interested. Come and check me out."

"Thanks." He stuffed the card inside his jacket. "I might just do that."

She smiled as she floated away.

GRAY'S HOUSEKEEPER gave Diana and Eric the grand tour of Gray's mansion and escorted them into the study to wait for him.

"Man." Eric sat beside her on the upholstered couch looking at the deluxe bookshelf full of hardbacks of romantic classics. "This dude is *not* getting all this dough from dealing art."

Diana sighed, crossing her legs.

"Be mad at me all you want." Eric sat with his legs wide open. "There was no way I would let you come here alone."

"It's just lunch."

"With a guy connected to the most dangerous drug lord in the United States. We agreed to do this my way, didn't we? Malton is a creep. He was all over you last night."

"Just like Pamela Peacock was all over *you*?"

"She was not."

"Oh, yes she was, and you didn't seem to mind it."

He laughed. "Are you jealous, Di?"

"You can cozy up to Pamela but I can't have lunch with Gray?"

"I don't give a damn about that woman, but if she can give me information that helps you then I'll do what I have to."

"That's exactly what I'm doing with Gray, and you're cramping my style, Eric. He's suspicious of our relationship. How am I going to get him to trust me with you hanging around?"

He darted his eyes toward her. "What do you mean he's suspicious of our relationship?"

"He thought we were together and when I said we weren't he didn't believe me."

His lips relaxed into a playful smile. "See, it's obvious how we feel about each other."

"It's over." She straightened the strap of her white summer dress. "We can't keep living in the past."

"You're my past and my future." He held her wrist. "I love you, Diana. I love you with all my heart and I can't let you go."

"Eric." She inhaled. "Please, stop."

"Then stop breaking my heart."

"Anna." Gray stood in the doorway, his smile disappearing when he looked at Eric. "Hello again, Mr. Carter."

Eric stood, closing his white blazer. "Mr. Malton. It's nice to see you again."

Gray's smile didn't hide his disdain.

"I hope you don't mind me tagging alone," Eric said.

Gray took Diana's hand and helped her from the couch. "You're even more beautiful than last night."

"Thank you. I like your shirt."

Lavender made his amber eyes sing.

"Did you enjoy the tour?" Gray asked.

Eric turned in a circle. "Your home is out of this world. A little stuffy for my tastes but classy."

Gray grimaced. "Maybe you just aren't used to this environment."

Diana held her breath as Eric's face flexed with aggression.

"I didn't mean to offend," he said. "It's just not my style."

Gray lifted his head, squinting. "No offense taken and I'm sorry if I was rude."

"No, you expected to be alone with Anna and I crashed the party."

"Then it was my fault," Diana said. "I should've told you Eric was coming."

"It's okay." Gray patted her back. "So here it is." He spread out his arms. "The room I've been aching for you to see."

Diana nodded. "It's lovely."

The three stood in silence, exchanging awkward glances.

"How about I leave you two alone," Eric said. "May I check out your pool, Gray?"

"Sure." His face remained neutral. "If you need anything, then let Elsie know."

Eric nodded at him, glanced at Diana and left the room.

"I'm sorry he came, Gray."

"No, no." He touched her chin. "I'm so glad you're here. I've been thinking about you since last night."

"Your home is just gorgeous." Diana walked to the glass case of miniature statues. "These are adorable. May I?"

"Sure."

She opened the door and picked up the little Greek soldier with his arm in the air. "This is incredible. Is this a scene from the Trojan War?"

"Uh-huh. You don't lie, do you, Anna?"

"Excuse me?"

"Are you sure nothing's going on between you and Eric?"

"We were together, but it's over. He's just very protective of me."

"You can take care of yourself." He moved in closer, rubbing his arm on hers. "Is there anyone else?" His voice cracked with desperation. "Are you single?"

"Yes, I am."

His faced turned the color of cayenne pepper.

"Isn't this Odysseus?" Diana studied the tiny statue.

He stared at her.

"Gray?"

"Hmm?" He shook his head. "Oh, sorry. Yes, that's Odysseus. You're into Greek Mythology?"

"Studied it in school and fell in love. How did they get such detail into something so tiny? Where's Achilles?"

Gray handed her the tiny hero. "Odysseus is my favorite."

"Why?"

"He was brilliant. After all, he came up with the trick that won the war."

"Odysseus was arrogant and selfish." She put Achilles back in the case. "He repeatedly risked lives to prove a point."

"He was a champion and he won the war." The muscles in Gray's cheeks contracted. "Isn't that what's important?"

She overlooked the collection. "Where's Helen?"

He kissed her hand. "Right here."

"Uh, what art did you want to show me?"

"You're different from the women I'm usually around." He kept her hand as she tried to move away. They only want men with power. If you can't do anything for them they have no need for you. I want a woman that knows what I can offer her."

She fidgeted. "I'm sure you'll find her one day."

"I believe I have."

"Slow down, okay?" She held her palm out to him. "I appreciate you helping me but we should stay on track. I came here to talk about art."

"Damn it." He stepped back, dropping his head. "I was too forward again. Please, accept my apology."

"It's fine as long as you understand why I'm here."

He tucked in his lips. "I do."

"Good. Now, where are the portraits you wanted to show me?"

CHAPTER SIX

"**Y**ou're gonna love this." Gray opened his walk-through closet stuffed with paintings and took out a portrait of the Appalachian Mountains.

Colors so vibrant the mountains moved before Diana's eyes.

Gray smiled wide. "What do you think?"

"My god, it's lovely."

"A very talented artist in China did it. She's one of the most revered new talents on the art scene." He looked at the painting, glowing. "I've sold her pieces to influential people, so you'd be in great company. Would it fit your collection?"

The portrait behind him charmed Diana. "What is that one?"

A gorgeous, olive-skinned woman with raven hair flowing like a river, stood in a sheer, white robe against a black background. Her Italian features stretched into a coy expression while she held one side of the robe open showing a peek of her teardrop breast.

Diana touched the brush strokes, staring into the young woman's fiery eyes.

"*Anna?*" Gray sang, standing closely behind her. "You smell amazing."

"I want this portrait."

"What?"

"This is breathtaking. It's like she's standing right here in front of us. I've seen nothing like it. Who is she?"

"Celestina Alfonso. She was an Italian model."

"Was?"

"She's dead now."

Diana touched the portrait. "What happened?"

"This was taken before she was killed two years ago."

"What happened?"

Gray didn't speak.

"She looks so young."

"She was probably about thirty here. This portrait was made from a photo taken about a month before she died. The portrait is a requested piece from the man who loved her. He searched for the best artist to give it justice and he found one in Belize. It just got in yesterday and I'll be taking it to the client soon."

"That's so romantic. This man must really love her."

"He paid a million to have it done. Paid for the artist's living arrangements while he completed it. It took about five months."

Diana touched the woman's face. "Who's the client?"

"Milan Vitale."

Jackpot.

"Maybe you've heard the name."

"Yes, and I know what he does but I want this portrait, Gray."

"No way." He guffawed. "Milan cherished Celestina, and she was the love of his life. He wouldn't give it up for nothing in the world."

"I want this portrait." She faced him, crossing her arms.

He set the other landscape portrait in the closet. "You can't afford it, dear."

"You said you'd give me a deal on anything I was interested in."

"Within reason."

"You expect me to walk away from such a remarkable piece? I don't care what I'd have to pay, but I want this portrait and I'm willing to fight for it."

"Against Milan Vitale?"

"I don't care. I can make a bid for it."

He sandwiched her hand in both of his. "I will get you any other painting in the world you'd like but I can't get you this one."

"I'm not giving up."

"Unless you talk to Milan about it yourself, I can't help you."

She grabbed her hips, beaming.

Mission accomplished.

"How do I reach Milan?"

"Anna." Gray rubbed the bridge of his nose as if she'd given him a headache. "You can't just walk off the street and meet Milan Vitale. He's very guarded for obvious reasons. The only way he'd agree to see you is if I took you to him and I'm not about to do that."

"Why not?"

"Because he's dangerous, and this is silly. No way in hell he'd give you that picture." He sat in the French style armchair and crossed his legs at the ankles. "I can't do it, Anna. I'm sorry."

"Well." She stuck her chin in the air. "I'll be going."

"Wait." He jumped in her path. "We haven't had lunch yet."

"I've lost my appetite."

"Come on." He caressed her arm, eyebrows pulling together. "Please, don't go."

"You said you'd help me and you wanted to make my time in Miami pleasurable. Did you mean that?"

"Yes."

"Take me to Milan or I'm going back to Los Angeles."

"I don't want his world to touch you."

"That's not your concern and I can take care of myself."

"You're stubborn." He rubbed the back of his head. "Fine. I have to deliver the painting in a few days. I'll take you."

She smiled.

"But he'll never let you have that portrait."

She wiggled her shoulders. "We'll see."

"THAT'S IT?" MILAN SIPPED fresh orange juice on the terrace of his gated patio surrounded by bodyguards. "You've got nothing?"

> "No one on my end has come up with any leads." Ivan Vitale crossed his legs. "But don't worry, Cousin. We'll find the leak like we always do."

Milan propped his elbows on the table and rubbed the fat ruby ring on his finger. "Before Father died, he felt like something was closing in on him. Like his time was up."

Ivan straightened the lace doily under his glass.

"I feel the same way. Like my time's running out."

"Chill, okay?" Ivan's bushy, dirty-blond brows flattened on his narrow forehead. "Let us handle this. Why don't you take a vacation? How about France?" He picked lint off his beige slacks. "You love Nice this time of year."

"George Wayans and that leak is all I'm concerned with right now."

"Why the hell hasn't Ramon found George yet?" Ivan took a cigar out of Milan's case and snapped his fingers at a guard.

He rushed to the table and lit the cigar for Ivan.

"Old Georgie Boy is elusive for sure." Ivan slipped the cigar between his droopy lips. "But no one's ever gotten away from us."

"And he won't either. I'll get George Wayans if I have to put a hit out on the whole fucking world. He is *not* getting away with what he's done."

Ivan's eyes narrowed behind his Versace shades. "Are you sure you can depend on Ramon?"

"What is with you and Douglas and this crusade you have against Ramon? He's never given me a reason to not trust him. Douglas even said he might be the leak." Milan laughed. "It's ridiculous. I can depend on Ramon more than I can depend on anyone else."

The aroma of high-quality tobacco escaped Ivan's lips. "Douglas and I aren't the only ones who feel this way."

Milan rolled his eyes.

"People have been talking throughout the organization. They question Ramon's loyalty to you and us. Some of them have even threatened to cut ties with the empire if you leave Ramon in charge."

"Are you questioning my father's judgement?"

"No." Ivan sat back. "I'd never question Uncle Luca but Ramon's not even family."

"He is to me. Ramon was like a second son to my father. He trusted Ramon with his life and he wouldn't hand the empire to just anyone. If something happens to me, Ramon *will* be leader and I don't care what you or anyone else thinks about it."

Ivan puffed, scoffing.

"I want George Wayans' head on a platter. Worry about that and not Ramon."

Ivan gave a blasé nod. "We'll find George."

CHAPTER SEVEN

A few days later, Diana and Eric stood with Gray on Milan's island-style veranda.

Bodyguards in sharp digs and shades protected the marble space.

"Milan," Gray said. "This is the beautiful woman I was telling you about, Anna Hampton. Anna, this is Milan Vitale."

Milan sat on the white sectional in front of the fireplace.

He glared at her, and the creases of his eyes might have aged another man but he made them an attribute.

"Hello, Miss Hampton." He held out his immaculate hand, which proved he hadn't done a day of hard labor in his life. "God, you've got the prettiest eyes."

"Doesn't she?" Gray giggled. "They look like little brown jewels."

Diana cringed.

"It's nice to meet you, Miss Hampton," Milan said.

"Um." Diana swallowed, wondering how many people he'd killed with that hand. "Nice to meet you too, Mr. Vitale."

Milan squeezed her hand, and she wasn't sure if he meant to hurt her but he had. "Do I make you nervous?"

"No." She managed a light chuckle. "But, I'd like to have my hand back the same way I gave it to you."

His face lit with amusement as he let go. "I don't know my strength."

Diana looked at Eric, rubbing her stinging hand.

"Hi." Eric offered his hand to Milan. "I'm Eric Carter. A friend of Diana's."

Milan shook Eric's hand with a strong, quick grip.

"Are you all right, Miss Hampton?" Milan gave her an underlook. "I didn't hurt you, did I?"

The question sounded like a warning. "No." She faked a smile. "I appreciate you agreeing to meet me. I'm sure you're busy."

"Not doing anything." He raised a ragged notepad with pages hanging out of it. "Just writing."

Diana held her hair back from the breeze. "What do you write?"

"Poetry." He grabbed a handful of grapes. "Please sit down and don't be nervous."

Gray helped Diana into a chair while Eric sat on the other side of her.

"I didn't know Mr. Carter would be joining us until I went to pick up Anna." Gray's phony smile looked as though someone stuck it on his face. "He has a habit of surprising people."

Eric's mouth twisted.

"Glad you came, Mr. Carter." Milan smiled.

"Thank you. Your home is gorgeous. I saw it in a home decorating magazine once."

"Yes, it's been in the family for generations. My parents cherished it. God rest their souls."

"How long have you been writing poetry?" Diana asked.

"Since I could write." Milan's eyes rolled back into his head. "It's my escape."

"With this palace you need an escape?" Eric asked.

"It takes more than money to make me happy. Feeding my soul with art and literature is a blessing. That's how I met Gray." Milan slapped Gray's hand. "A love of art." Milan's phone beeped, he checked it, and smiled at Diana. "I'll deal with this later."

"If it's important, please don't let us hold you up," she said.

"No, I can deal with it after this. Rwanda will still be there."

The maids brought out fruit trays and orange juice.

Eric thanked the maid for his juice and asked, "Rwanda?"

"There's a school in a village there that's being closed down," Milan said. "It's the only one in the area and the children will have nothing."

"That's horrible," Diana said.

"Heartbreaking," Milan said. "They're losing funding so I'll donate some money and send a crew down there to build another one."

"Hold on." Eric gaped. "You're building a school in Rwanda on a whim?"

"Why not? I have the money and the kids need schooling. I give to charities all the time and I love children."

Diana looked at Eric whose mouth hung open.

"Surprised?" Milan asked as the maids brought out cheese trays. "Thought I was just some tyrant who didn't care about anyone?"

Diana twitched. "No."

"Bullshit."

"Maybe I shouldn't have come here."

"Why?" Milan chewed pineapple chunks. "Because I'm making you uncomfortable?"

"Yes and you seem to be enjoying it."

"I've insulted you?" Milan chewed with a frisky glare. "Don't take it personally. I can be a tricky bastard when I want to be. Ask Gray."

Gray held a shaky smile while Eric stared at the fruit in front of him.

"Be straight with me, Miss Hampton," Milan said. "And I will do the same with you."

"Okay." She sat erect, wiggling her neck. "I'm surprised a man like you would care about people in need considering the pain you've put people through."

"Judging me on business decisions?"

"Business decisions?" She grimaced. "Is that what you call it?"

Eric took her arm. "Anna—"

"Yes, that's what I call it," Milan said. "What do *you* call it?"

"I call it madness." She rested her elbows on the table. "Cruelty, sinful, vicious. Shall I go on?"

"Anna." Gray put his arm around her chair. "You don't talk that way to Milan."

"Why not? He's just a person like I am." She looked into his suffocating eyes. "He said he wanted me to be straight, well I'm being straight. You're a horrible human being who preys on people to get what you want."

"Anna," Gray snapped.

"Is all you see a criminal, Miss Hampton?" Milan leaned forward, wiggling his fingers. "Blood on my hands from the many people I've killed? The pain that I've caused and the lives I've wrecked?"

"If you were in my shoes, wouldn't that be what *you* saw?"

He glanced at his guards, sat back and rubbed his nose. "Mr. Carter, you're quiet."

"I..." Eric stuffed a square of Irish cheddar cheese in his mouth.

"Do you agree with Miss Hampton?" Milan tilted his head. "Am I the monster she says I am?"

"You've done horrible things." Eric chewed. "Can't blame people for judging you because of them."

Diana smiled.

"I like you, Mr. Carter." Milan stroked his ring. "You're a straight shooter, no bullshit. I could tell it when I shook your hand. You had a firm grip, and it shows you say what you mean and mean what you say."

"Well, I try to."

Diana's eyes met Milan's. "Do you want me to go?"

He covered his mouth with his hand but she could tell by how the creases lifted around his eyes he was smiling. "No."

She put her hands in her lap, palms sticking together from sweat. "Why not?"

"I never walk away from a challenge."

"Is that what I am?"

"Oh, yes." He lowered his hand. "Probably the biggest challenge I've encountered in a long time."

Gray grumbled, ripping a wedge of cheese in half.

Milan's tongue peeked from his lips as he spoke to Diana, "It'll be fun changing your mind about me."

"Why don't we get to the painting?" Gray asked. "Isn't that why we're here?"

"Sure." Milan placed his napkin on his plate and stood. "Follow me."

"Mr. Vitale?" Eric stood, wiping his mouth. "Could I look around if you don't mind? Your home is unbelievable."

"Sure. You can relax at the pool. Take a load off. Henry?" Milan gestured to the guard lounging on the daybed looking at his phone. "Henry?"

He looked up, raising his shades. "Yes, sir?"

"For God's sakes you're on your phone more than a teenage girl. Show Mr. Carter to the pool area."

Henry jumped up. "Right this way, Mr. Carter."

Eric gave Diana a cautionary glance and left with Henry.

Some guards went inside with Milan while the others watched over Diana and Gray.

Gray pulled her close. "Listen."

"Don't grab me like that." She snatched away from him. "What's wrong with you?"

"He's manipulating you already. Don't fall into his trap."

"Move." She pushed him. "If Milan is so terrible then why are you all up under him? He's fine when you're getting his money or whatever other perks from hanging around him."

He gnashed his teeth. "You don't know what you're talking about."

She rolled her eyes and entered the mansion.

CHAPTER EIGHT

"Man, this is something else." Eric rested on the lounge chair by the super-sized, square pool.

Henry sat on the other seat, his gun dangling from his skinny waist.

"If you need to do something, it's fine," Eric said. "I'll wait out here until Anna's done."

"I gotta stay out here," Henry mumbled with his face in his phone. "It's for protection."

"What do I need protection from?"

Henry lowered the phone, grimacing. "Not for you, for Mr. Vitale." His phone rang and he checked the call. "Excuse me." He got up and headed toward the cabana.

"Thank god." Eric laid his head back and closed his eyes.

A moment later a towel swept across his face.

"Hey." He opened his eyes to Pam glowing in the sun in a black bikini that seemed to shrink the longer he looked at it. "Jesus."

She hung the towel over her shoulder, covering her tattoo. "What do we have here? How are you today, officer?"

"Now I get it." Eric sat up straight. "Singing at his club, hanging with his friends, you're Milan's girl, aren't you? But I heard he doesn't have just one so you're a part of his collection?"

She frowned. "You're wrong."

He squinted from the sun. "It doesn't look that way to me."

"Milan is my friend. He took me under his wing."

He gazed at her legs. "I bet he did."

"It's nothing romantic between us." She sat, crossing her legs. "It's your turn, officer. Why are you hanging around?"

"I'm not a cop."

"Okay." She clicked her jaw. "Whatever you say. What do you want with Milan though?"

"Pam?" A black guy with dreads past his shoulders and muscles popping from his shirt, approached. "What's up?" He eyed Eric.

"Douglas." Pam stood, pulling her bikini out her crack. "Is everything okay?"

"Who are you?" he asked Eric.

"Who are *you*?"

Douglas raised his shirt to show the gun on his waist. "I asked you first."

"Eric Carter this is Douglas Paul." Pam clutched Douglas' chest. "It's okay. He's a friend of Gray's new lady friend."

Douglas checked out Pam's bikini and gave her a tender kiss on the cheek. "We need to talk later."

"I'm singing at the club Friday night." She touched his dreads. "You gonna come?"

"I don't know. Milan might have something for me to do."

Her mouth drooped. "Well, we'll talk later."

He pinched her cheek and glared at Eric as he left.

"I was wrong," Eric teased. "You're Douglas' girl?"

"Why do you care who I'm with? What?" She held her waist. "You want me?"

"Don't flatter yourself."

"What do you want then?"

"Ah, there she is!" A tall, olive-toned man who reminded Eric of a slippery con artist, grabbed Pam and swung her around, his bracelets clinking. "Ooh wee, you look so fine."

"Ramon." She pushed at his firm arms. "Stop."

"Girl," he growled, with a gap in his two front teeth. "Being away from you even a day is too much." He pushed against her, his necklace tangling in that thick black forest on his chest. "Feel that dick," he whispered. "You miss that?"

"*Ramon.*" She looked at Eric.

Ramon let her go, his curly black hair primped into a stylish pompadour. "Haven't had the pleasure of meeting your new friend."

"This is Eric Carter," Pam said. "He's a friend of Anna Hampton's. Gray's new lady friend. She came to see Milan about a painting."

Ramon grabbed Eric's hand and did one of those smooth handshakes with a ring on every finger. "Ramon Sotolongo. Nice to meet you."

"You too." Eric massaged his hand afterwards to get the feeling back.

"Come on, Pam." Ramon grabbed her hand. "I need to talk."

"You don't wanna talk."

He snatched her ass. "This dick wants to talk."

She pushed at him. "Stop, okay?"

"She doesn't seem too interested," Eric interjected. "Maybe you should cool it."

Ramon shoved Pam behind him. "You should mind your own fuckin' business."

"It's hard to when someone is being an asshole to a lady."

"What you say?" Ramon cracked his knuckles. "Get your ass up and say it to my face, faggot."

"Ramon, stop." Pam jumped in front of him. "I told you about your anger."

"Fuck you," he told Eric.

"No thanks." Eric snickered. "Looks like nobody else around here wants to either."

Ramon muttered under his breath, grabbed Pam, and pulled her toward the house.

Douglas walked out to the corridor as they approached.

Ramon said something to Pam that Eric couldn't hear, and she scurried off in the opposite direction.

Eric snuck toward the house and ducked behind a podium to hear Douglas and Ramon's conversation.

"You got any news to report?" Douglas asked.

Ramon lit a cigarette. "Get the fuck out my face. I don't report to you."

Douglas knocked Ramon's cigarette out his mouth and stomped on it. "I'm not playing games with your dumb ass. Now have you found George Wayans yet?"

"I got my boys on it so don't worry about it."

"Yeah well your boys are fucking up. They ain't come up with shit and it's been weeks. You've found witnesses in protective custody but can't find George?"

"I'll find him." Ramon lit another cigarette. "Focus on your own shit."

"Instead of chasing after Pam all the damn time, your ass needs to be doing your job."

"Course this is about Pam again. Oh, Dougie." Ramon tapped Douglas' cheek and Douglas smacked his hand. "She's made her choice and she chose me."

"You don't give a damn about Pam. You're just with her because I want her."

Eric's forehead rose.

"Face it, Douglas. I'm the better man around here. Pam knows it, the organization knows it and Milan knows it. All this is because you're jealous that I get to be leader if something happened to Milan."

"Wouldn't surprise me if something suddenly happened with you next in line."

"You better shut your mouth. Milan's like a brother to me."

"Is that right, *Cain*?"

Ramon chuckled. "Maybe you should take a job at Milan's club doing standup comedy."

"No one's fooled by your ass except Milan and I'll make sure he sees the truth."

"Watch it, Dougie." Ramon whistled. "You're on my list."

Douglas walked away. "Bring it, motherfucker."

CHAPTER NINE

"Enlighten me, Miss Hampton." Milan walked across the frost-gray carpet of his parlor, the sun from the floor-to-ceiling windows igniting the white décor. "Why would you want something so sentimental to someone else?"

"Because it's the most beautiful thing I've seen in my life." Diana tried to scoot over on the couch but Gray sat so close he had her pinned to the pillows. "But, I'm sure I can't meet your price."

"You never know." Milan sat in the Victorian-style chair behind the desk and opened the jar of lemon drops. "Make me an offer."

"Gray told me you paid a million dollars."

That goofy, lovesick smile returned to Gray's face every time she looked at him.

"I don't have that kind of money."

"If you did..." Milan sucked the candy. "Would you pay it?"

"I love art." She touched her bosom. "I breathe it. It relaxes me and challenges me at the same time. I love learning about an artist just from looking at their work. There's a bond that forms that's like nothing else."

Milan slipped the entire drop into his mouth.

"Art brings me peace I can't get anywhere else. It's like an addiction."

"That's how I feel about writing." Milan smiled. "I get a pencil and my notepad and I'm in my world. I can have any adventure I want. Do anything I want. Go anywhere I want."

"Don't you do that now?" Diana asked.

"No." His face dropped and color left his cheeks.

"I can tell from what Gray said how much you loved Celestina. A woman's lucky to have a man feel that way about her."

Gray tapped his thumbs together.

"My yacht's named after her too." Milan pointed to a photo of a luxury ship behind his head. "This is the *Celestina*."

Diana took in the masterpiece. "I love it."

"Anna loved my yacht too." Gray pulled her close. "Didn't you? You kept raving about it."

She pushed his arm away.

Gray frowned, clearing his throat. "Are you selling her the painting or not?"

Milan took a cigar box out the desk drawer. "She hasn't made me an offer yet."

"I've changed my mind."

"What?" Gray asked.

"You were right, Gray," Diana said. "How can I buy something that means so much to him? No way I'd cherish it like he would."

Milan's cheeks reddened as he took a hit of the cigar. "As if you wanted the painting anyway."

She batted her eyes. "Excuse me?"

"You just wanted to meet me." His tone sounded raspier than usual. "To see just how evil I can be?"

"I admit, a part of me wanted to know more about a man who would make such a gesture for the woman he loved."

"Thought you already had me figured out."

"You were right on the veranda." She smiled. "You can't always judge someone from things you've heard."

"I've already gotten to you and it's just our first meeting." Milan nodded. "Can't wait until our next one."

He and Diana exchanged grins.

Gray raised his head. "What next meeting?"

Milan flicked ashes in the tray. "How long are you going to be in Miami, Anna?"

"I'm not sure."

"You have a cell number where I may reach you?"

"Sure."

"Why would you need her number?" Gray asked.

"Did Mr. Carter get lost?" Milan set the cigar in the ashtray and headed for the door. "I'll see where he is."

"I'm sure he's fine." Diana scooted to the edge of the couch. "Your home is a wonder. Something probably caught his attention."

Milan smiled at her as he opened the door. "It's easy to get lost around here. I'll be right back." He left.

Gray seized Diana's wrist. "What's going on between you and Milan?"

"Excuse me?"

"That flirting. You're playing with fire."

"We were just talking, Gray."

"Did you see how he was looking at you? Listen—"

"Stop grabbing me. You act like I belong to you and I don't like it."

"I apologize." He moved his hands around as if he didn't know what to do with them. "I can't help how I feel around you."

"You need to back off."

"Milan's like a wild animal. He's more dangerous when wounded."

"What?"

"He's vulnerable right now. A lot of shit's going on in the organization not to mention his dad's death."

"I thought his father had been sick for years." Diana moved her hair off her shoulder. "I know it's painful to lose a parent but he must've been prepared."

Gray took a breath. "It's the way Luca died that's the issue."

"He died from dementia."

"That's what the public thinks, but it isn't true. Someone poisoned him."

"What?"

"You can't tell anyone."

"Does Milan know who did it?"

"Maybe." Gray propped his arm on the back of the sofa. "May I have a kiss now?"

"I gotta go to the bathroom." She stood. "I've been holding it since we came in here."

"There's a restroom down the hall." He pointed to the door, gawking at her legs. "Just turn left at that statue and it's the first door you see."

She tottered to the door. "I'll be right back."

He blew her a kiss. "I'll be waiting."

She rolled her eyes, shut the door and scurried through the hall until she came to the statue. She smiled at a passing bodyguard and rushed into the bathroom greeted by a golden oasis of Italian furniture.

She sat on the edge of the black tub trimmed in gold and called Eric.

"Hey," he answered.

"Where are you?"

"Upstairs in the library. This place is huge. You need a map to find the next room."

"Could you search anything?"

"Are you kidding? I can barely move with Henry up my ass. If I farted he'd smell it before it came out."

"Milan's looking for you." Diana walked to the sink. "Did you find out anything about my father?"

"I heard these two guys Douglas and Ramon arguing about George but nothing else."

"What were they saying?"

"Apparently Ramon's supposed to be looking for George and Douglas thinks he's slacking on the job."

"Shit." Diana leaned forward on the black marble vanity.

"Anything on your end?"

"Nah, but Milan's warming up to me. Gray's getting too clingy. Gotta get rid of his ass."

Someone knocked on the door.

"Anna, are you all right?"

"Fuck." She stood straight. "It's Gray. I can't even go to the bathroom without him bugging me."

"Anna?"

"I'm all right," she yelled. "I'll be out in a minute!" She muttered into the phone, "God. I've had enough of these people today. Let's get the hell out of here. Meet me in Milan's parlor."

Eric chuckled. "If I can find it."

Diana exited the bathroom and bumped into a Herculean black man with chiseled features and a tight shirt that hugged his pecs.

"Hey." His dreads dangled in front of his royal eyes. "You're Miss Hampton, right? I'm Douglas Paul. I work for Milan."

She shook his massive, ashy hand. "Nice to meet you."

He stared at her, rubbing his mouth.

"What?"

"You're not what I expected." He beamed with photogenic teeth. "How in the world did Gray get a woman like you?"

"Hold on. He hasn't gotten anything over here." She straightened her dress. "He was helping me get some art for my collection."

"You need to tell him that because he acts like you guys are getting married."

"That ain't *never* happening."

Douglas covered his grin.

"Anna." Milan walked toward them with Eric. "I found Mr. Carter coming off the elevator. You met Douglas, huh? Is everything okay?"

"I need to speak to you, Milan," Douglas said. "It's important."

"Don't be rude, Douglas. You see I have guests. Did he give you the third degree, Anna? Don't mind him, he's very protective."

"No, he was a gentleman."

Douglas smiled.

Gray hurried toward them, his pants twisting at the crotch. "There you are." He squeezed in between Diana and Milan and took her hand. "Are you ready to go? I'm sure Milan has business to take care of. He's a busy man."

"It was nice to meet you, Milan."

He took Diana's hand with a warmness she hadn't expected. "It was a pleasure, and I'm sorry if I hurt your hand before." He kissed it.

"It's okay."

"I have an idea. There's an art exhibit at the downtown museum Friday night. Would you like to come?"

Gray interjected, "I was planning to show Anna around town Friday."

"Really?" she asked. "Because I wasn't aware of this."

Milan smirked.

Gray smiled, putting her arm around her shoulders. "I said we could take a tour together."

"I must've forgotten." She unwrapped Gray's arm from her shoulders. "I'd rather go to the exhibit if you don't mind."

Gray clamped his teeth together. "It's your decision."

Eric cleared his throat, looking at Diana from the corner of his eyes.

"We're on then, Anna?" Milan asked.

"Sure." The butterflies in Diana's stomach multiplied. "I'd love to go."

Gray grumbled as he rocked in place.

Douglas snickered. "You okay there, Gray?"

"I'm fine." He crossed his arms like a scolded child. "Mind your own business."

Douglas chuckled as he walked away.

"I'll be at your hotel around seven," Milan said. "Mr. Carter, would you like to join us?"

Diana glared at him, warning him not to throw another wrench in her plan to get close to Milan.

"Um, no." He rubbed his hands. "Art's not really my thing. You two go ahead."

"All right." Milan beamed. "We'll have a wonderful time, Anna."

Diana nodded. "I look forward to it."

"Milan?" Gray lifted his chin. "Can I speak to you for a second? Anna, Mr. Carter, please wait for me at the car."

CHAPTER TEN

Gray followed Milan into the parlor and slammed the door.

"You seem angry, Gray." Milan stood by the desk with his arms crossed. "Did I do something?"

"I respect you, and I appreciate everything you've done for me. But I'm not going down this road again."

"What road is that?"

"I'm asking you to stay away from Anna. She's mine."

Milan sniggered, scratching his hairy cheek. "Wow."

"I'm not budging on this."

"Woof!" Milan threw up his fists, cackling. "It's hilarious watching you strut around with your tail in the air."

"That's all I am to you and everyone around here, a joke."

"Gray." Milan sat on the edge of his desk. "Anna Hampton is no more interested in you than she is in the grass outside."

"What did you say?"

"If you paid attention to a woman's signals instead of the fantasy in your head, your heart wouldn't keep getting broken. You always come on way too strong, scare the woman off and then blame me."

He charged the desk. "No, what happens is they meet the great Milan and then they pitch me to the side like trash. It's not happening this time. Other women might run to your money and power but Anna isn't like that."

Milan raised his eyebrow. "Sure about that?"

"Yes. I won't let you steal her like you stole everyone else."

"Are you forgetting who you're talking to?" The wrinkles in Milan's forehead deepened. "With a snap of my fingers, your world could come crashing down. You're nothing without me, Gray. Hell, you're nothing anyway, but I make you less of a nothing than you already are."

Gray clenched fists, digging his fingernails into his palms.

"What? You wanna hit me?" Milan got closer to him with that patronizing smirk he seemed to save for Gray. "Look. I'm gonna take it easy on you because you're not thinking. Never talk to me like this again. Do you hear me?"

Gray swallowed his anger, remembering Milan could ruin his life or *take* it with the blink of an eye. "I wasn't trying to be disrespectful. I just like her. This might be real."

"Remember where your loyalties lie." Milan tapped Gray's cheek. "As for Anna, if she's really interested in you then I can't steal her, right?"

"TALK TO ME," DIANA whispered in the backseat of the Lincoln Navigator Black Label as Gray's driver took her and Eric back to their hotel.

Eric stared ahead, shaking his leg.

Diana scooted closer to him so the driver couldn't hear. "Did I do something?"

"If I told you not to go out with Milan, would you respect that?"

"How am I going to find out why he's looking for my father if I don't spend time with him?"

He scoffed. "He's sucking you in already."

"That's ridiculous. You sound like Gray."

"Gray's right."

"I'm playing a part, Eric."

"You're no match for him, Diana. It was obvious."

They passed neighborhoods with posh condos surrounded by palm trees and pristine lawns.

A sarcastic grin peeked from Eric's lips. "I saw how your face lit up when you saw Milan's place."

"Enough."

"The wonderment in your eyes when you spoke to him."

"What are you saying?" She dug her fingers into the leather seats. "That I like Milan? The man is a murderer. He disgusts me and I'm offended you'd suggest otherwise."

"You want a taste of what Milan can give you." His lips quivered. "Admit it."

"I don't care about money."

"What woman wouldn't want what he could give?"

"*Me,*" she snapped in a whisper. "I want nothing from Milan except answers."

He looked ahead again. "It killed me, Diana."

"What?"

"Watching how enamored you were and knowing I could never give you that." He exhaled through his nostrils. "Made me feel so inadequate."

"Eric." She touched his hand. "Milan isn't half the man you are."

"I always wanted to give you the best because that's what you deserve."

"What is this about?" She stopped touching him. "You seem so broken."

"I've been broken since we split up but this is the first time I felt like I've lost you." Water gathered on his bottom eyelids. "I always thought I'd get you back, now I'm not so sure."

She went to touch him again but he pulled back.

"Am I right, Di?" He looked at her with an aching that tore her soul to pieces. "Have I lost you forever?"

She turned away having no idea what to say.

DIANA AND MILAN VIEWED the spectacular showings at the show while chatting with the featured artists. Everyone seemed more impressed with Milan than the art. He could demand attention and respect in any setting.

They examined the towering rock sculpture painted in dark, melancholy hues. "Are you having a nice time?" Milan asked.

"Nice doesn't describe it." Diana sipped champagne. "I'm on top of the world."

People took pictures of the exhibits with their cell phones.

"Do you have plans after this?" Milan drank from his glass. "Going out with Gray?"

"Not tonight." She pulled the Chiffon shawl over her shoulders. "Why?"

"Come home with me."

She held her breath.

"We can have dinner together."

She clasped her quivering hands. "Alone?"

"Well, besides the servants. I wanna get to know you better or are you too afraid to let that happen?"

"I'm not afraid of you."

As long as I got my gun on me.

"I'm surprised by the invitation." She tilted her head, laying the coyness on thick. "Because you didn't seem to like me when we met and now you want to have dinner with me?"

"I didn't squeeze your hand because I didn't like you. I did it to send a message."

"Pain is a message?"

"A powerful one." He flexed his shoulders in the white, Tom Ford blazer. "One people don't forget."

"I don't like hurting people."

"Neither do I." He smiled, tapping his glass against hers.

"When I think I got you figured out, you confuse me again."

He laughed. "Then I'm doing my job." He touched the curve of her back, whispering, "What do you want from me, Anna?"

She trembled with electricity from his touch. "I was about to ask you the same question."

"All I want is dinner with you." He got closer, breathing on her nose. "At least for now."

CHAPTER ELEVEN

D iana sunk into the polyester cushions of the wicker sectional in the center of Milan's garden. "That crab was delicious."

"Just got it in today." He sat beside her, slumped over with his face glued to his tattered notepad. "Glad you liked it."

Diana tapped her fingers on the arm of the sofa, the bright yellow flowers with bell-shaped petals catching her eye. "What are those?"

"Allamanda," Milan muttered while writing.

"How did you know which ones I meant since you're not paying attention?"

"Because every time someone comes out here, they ask what those are." He smiled at her. "And, I am paying attention."

"Doesn't seem like it." She laid her shawl in her lap. "This is the first time a man's invited me back to his place and ignored me."

"I'm sorry." He lifted his head. "When I get ideas, I have to write or I lose them."

"Is this where you always write? Do you come out here every night?"

"Yes. The garden brings me peace." He glanced at the thick, purple-black sky. "I can think and people leave me alone."

"What about before you go to sleep? Do you write in your bedroom? Is there any place *inside* you like to write?"

He sighed, wriggling his shoulders.

"You're playing a game with me, aren't you?"

He turned to another blank page and wrote. "I'd say you're the one who's playing games. Why are you here, Anna? Better yet, what do you want from me?"

"You invited me here. I thought for company but it's looking more like an interrogation."

"Sorry, but I don't trust many people. I can't." He tapped the pad with his pencil. "Everyone wants something from me so why should you be any different?"

"What I want is for you to stop being so suspicious of me."

"Can't do it." He shook his head. "I can't let my guard down around you or anyone." He turned toward her. "My dad stepped down from the organization when I was only twenty-three-years-old due to his health."

"I'm sorry for your loss by the way."

"I had to grow up fast. Imagine being that young, not even ever having a job then suddenly you're in charge of one of the most powerful empires in the world." He propped up his knee. "I wasn't ready for this life. A life of violence where

you have to kill someone else to survive. On top of that, I inherited my father's enemies. I was dodging bullets from every direction. Not just from his enemies but people in the Vitale Empire who didn't want me to be leader."

"Why didn't they?"

"Because *they* wanted the power. In the mafia, power is everything, Anna. I worked hard to get the respect of these people. It wasn't handed to me."

She dangled her sandal off her toes. "What did you do to get this respect?"

"Anything I had to." He pressed his lips together. "Without apologies or remorse. That's how it is in my world."

"How was Celestina killed?"

He squinted.

"I apologize if I'm prying."

He started writing again, the gold lights shining upon him as if he were a majestic figure.

"I get you, Milan. I understand what it's like to be you now." Her feet slid against the bronze ceramic tile. "They see this estate, your money and your looks and they think you have it all but it's the opposite, isn't it?"

He batted his eyes.

"What people envy about you is what you don't like the most. God, I can see it, Milan. I see *you*. The real you and you're lonely."

He flinched, his nose wet.

"This estate is your prison. You can't go anywhere without a bodyguard. You can't meet new people for fear they're working for an enemy. Someone always wants to take you out so can't trust anyone. I get it, Milan." She leaned into him. "I'm sorry you were forced into this life."

"Nice speech. Am I supposed to trust you now? Hand over the family jewels?"

"I want nothing from you, Milan."

"Bullshit. We all want something, Anna." His jaw set. "I like you."

"Did Celestina have a problem with your business?"

"No. She chose to be a part of it." He eased his grip on the pad. "You're a very attractive woman."

"Thank you."

"What's going on between you and Gray?"

"Nothing."

"He bit my head off the other day and told me to stay away because you were his."

Diana gaped. "No he *didn't*."

"Yes, he did. I told him you don't feel the same way about him. Am I wrong?"

She shook her head. "I thought he was nice at first but I see things in him that tell me I shouldn't have gotten involved with him."

"Gray's very insecure. He doesn't have my confidence or style."

The breeze tickled the end of her maxi dress. "Arrogant much?"

He nibbled on the pencil eraser. "It's not arrogance if it's true."

Diana checked her watch. "It's getting late. I'd better go."

"You don't have to." He set the pad and pencil on the aluminum table and took her wrist. "Your skin's so soft. It's like my hand can go right through it." He slipped his fingers between hers.

Her knees knocked but she hoped he didn't notice.

"Do you want to know the real me?"

She swam inside his eyes. "Yes, but I'm confused."

He inched his mouth toward hers, the rosy notes of Dom Perignon lingering on his breath. "What are you confused about?" His eyebrows lowered as he gripped her hip.

"This. One minute you act like you don't want me around and the next you're paying me compliments. Is this what it's going to always be like with you?"

"Stay and find out." He slipped his hand behind her head, tilted her until he got the angle he wanted and kissed her.

She whimpered, pushing against his chest but he held her in place.

She felt the creases of his lips against hers, becoming more familiar with him as a man the longer they smooched.

Diana put her arms around him as he sunk his sticky tongue further into her mouth. She hadn't imagined it would feel this good for a man she despised to want her.

Milan released her with a soft smack, sucking his lips clean as if to savor every drop of her. "That was some kiss."

"Yes." She fanned her boiling face. "I certainly didn't expect it."

He wrapped his long fingers around her waist. "I didn't expect it to feel so good—"

"Uh, I gotta go." She stood, wobbling from the aftermath of the kiss. "I've had a wonderful time, but would you please have your driver take me back to my hotel now?"

He stood. "Come back tomorrow."

She wrapped her shawl on her shoulders. "Is that a demand or invite?"

He wiped her raspberry lipstick off his mouth. "I only take volunteers for this assignment."

"Then I'll be back."

"Good. Maybe then I'll figure out what you want." He passed her, rubbing his crotch against her ass. "I'll get the driver."

CHAPTER TWELVE

"**E**rnesto's dead?" Milan walked with Douglas through the stone walkway in the garden the next day. "Are you sure?"

Douglas nodded. "Laying in a morgue in Atlanta, Georgia."

Milan's rubber soles glided across the tile. "Any word on how it happened?"

Douglas shook his head.

"Did he take care of George's daughter?"

"We don't know." Douglas massaged his huge knuckles. "Want me to send someone to her place to check it out?"

"Nah." Milan walked with his hands clasped behind his back. "George is what's important."

"Still no word?" Douglas parted his grinning lips. "What a surprise."

"Ramon's doing the best he can."

They passed the stunning, pink Gerbera daisies, Milan sniffing their perfumery scent.

"Ramon has it handled." Milan bumped Douglas with his elbow by accident. "Worry about what you need to."

"Doesn't look like he's handling shit but I'll drop it."

"Good." Milan pushed his hands in his pockets, the fresh greenery keeping Anna on his mind. "It's a beautiful day, isn't it? The sun's shining brighter. The birds are singing louder."

Douglas watched him from the corner of his eye, eyebrow rising.

"I never take the time to just enjoy what I have. People would kill to be in my shoes."

"I'd ask how your date with Anna went but judging by that goofy grin it went very well."

Milan chuckled, dropping his head.

"I'd be happy for you under different circumstances."

Milan halted, stopping Douglas along the way. "Spit it out."

"Anna Hampton and Eric Carter just pop up out of nowhere and it's fine? You're not suspicious?"

"We did background checks on them, remember? They seem to be who they say they are."

"But what do they want?"

Milan continued walking.

"You're very vulnerable right now and you have to keep your guard up."

Milan stopped again. "I was born with my guard up."

"I'm worried. You seem taken by her already."

Milan rocked his head as he continued walking. "Never was one to pass up a game with a beautiful woman."

"We need to be extra careful."

"Don't worry about me." Milan inhaled. "Worry about finding George and the damn traitor who's leaking to the FBI. I can handle Anna."

"Hmm." Douglas swayed. "I hope so before she handles you."

ERIC WALKED ALONG THE wooden docks and stopped at the houseboat with the redwood planks and golden doorknocker.

This didn't seem to fit a woman like Pam. She carried herself as if she were a Hilton yet lived on a houseboat?

Eric hopped on deck and peeked inside the window in her door.

Thrown furniture and scattered papers were everywhere.

He knocked. "Pam?"

"Who the hell is it?" She stomped toward the door, the boat rocking from her gait. "Get off my boat!"

"It's Eric Carter. Uh, may I talk to you?"

She popped out of the door with a rifle.

Eric jumped back and threw up his hands. "Whoa."

"What the hell are you doing here? Get off my boat."

"Why are you wielding a gun like Annie Oakley? What the hell's going on around here?"

"You're a man," she grumbled, lowering the gun. "I'm sick of men. How did you know where I lived?"

"Asked around."

"Why are you so interested in me? This game you got going is getting boring, Eric. What are you after?"

"Nothing that would hurt you or cause you harm."

"You're a fed, aren't you?"

"No. Why don't you put the gun down so we can talk?"

She did, and he followed her inside the boat and closed the door. "What happened, Pam?" He walked over scattered DVDs and a broken vase. "Are you in trouble?"

She touched the small bruise under the collar of her robe.

"Did someone attack you?"

"What do you care?"

He took the gun from her and laid it on the table. "Did one of Milan's men do this? Ramon?"

She shook her head, running her fingers through her short, spikey hair.

"Douglas?"

"Douglas would never hurt me." Her face constricted as if she struggled not to cry. "Some guy who works for Pablo Delgado."

"Jesus. The coke king?"

"Delgado wanted to send me a message."

Eric got the lamp from the floor and set it on the end table by her loveseat. "Pablo Delgado is one of the biggest coke dealers in the world."

"Delgado and Milan are on the verge of closing a huge deal." Pam held her robe closed. "They want to link empires, and Milan's determine to make it happen. The future of the empire depends on it."

"Thought Milan owned the south."

"Let's just say new players have come into the southern drug market and Milan's afraid of losing his place at the top. A deal with Delgado's cartel would solve all Milan's problems."

"What does this have to do with you?"

"I'm part of the deal." She walked across to the kitchen on bare feet. "Delgado has a thing for me." She got a glass out the cabinet above her counter. "He saw me singing at the club and since then I can't get him to leave me alone. He sends me gifts, he calls me. When I didn't respond how he wanted, he started threatening me. I told Milan, but all he cares about is the deal." She filled the glass with tap water. "Delgado's man was waiting here when I got home."

Eric blew a breath, wiping his mouth.

"He told me to get pretty, and he'd take me to Delgado, and I told him to go to hell and get off my boat." She exhaled. "He manhandled me and trashed my place. I got my gun, and he left."

He entered the kitchen. "Are you all right?"

She gulped after drinking. "It's not the first time a guy got rough with me."

"You need to go to the hospital?"

"No."

"Ramon isn't protecting you?"

She scoffed, tying her robe tighter. "He doesn't like that Delgado wants me but he'll keep quiet for the deal. Don't you get it? It's all about the empire with them. Nothing else matters."

Eric kneeled in the living room and picked up the papers from the floor and stacked them on her table.

She rushed out the kitchen. "You don't have to do that."

"I want to."

She grinned, sitting on the loveseat. "You definitely aren't like the men I usually come across."

"I don't care what Milan's done for you, you're not his property."

"Milan helped me when I had nothing. If not for him no telling where I'd be." She smiled. "He gave me a place to sing and I love singing more than anything. Besides, Douglas keeps me going. Just being around him is a reward. Ever met someone like that?"

Eric closed his eyes and Diana's warm smile appeared. "Yeah."

"Miss Hampton?" She touched her mouth, studying him. "Or should I say Diana Wayans?"

Eric got off his knees, gaping at her.

CHAPTER THIRTEEN

"**I**t's okay," Pam said. "I won't say anything."

"Fuck." Eric sat on the table. "How did you know?"

"Saw a picture of her once." She examined her black stiletto nails. "George showed me."

"How did George get involved with people like this?"

"The same way I did. Luck of the draw. Things happen where you don't have a choice and it's best to sleep *with* the devil than not. Now are you going to be honest with me and tell me who you really are?"

"Eric Sachs. I'm a Detective with the Atlanta PD."

"Knew it." She bobbed her head. "You got that 'cop' look."

"Diana's my friend."

"She's more than *that*." She flexed her fingers. "You're in love with her. It's plain as the nose on your face."

"Yeah, well it doesn't matter because it's over."

"But does she still want you?" Pam crossed her inviting legs. "If so that's something to fight for."

"I appreciate the romantic advice but where is George?"

"Your guess is as good as mine. He could be in Timbuktu or somewhere. He's been all over the freaking world."

"How can someone stay off the radar so well?"

"I'm sure he's fine. One thing George can do is take care of himself."

"He sure as hell never took care of his daughter."

"My dad was the same way. Never in the picture and I turned out like shit because of it." She clutched the armrest of the chair. "Diana at least had a mother, stepfather and good upbringing. I didn't have any of that." She straightened her shoulders. "George regrets the mistakes he's made with her but he doesn't know how to fix it."

"He can start by not being a damn coward. So Milan might know who she is?"

"Uh-uh." Pam picked at her fingernails. "She wouldn't be breathing if he did. You either. My advice, go back to Atlanta while you still can."

"Diana is stubborn. She won't stop until she finds out the truth and I'm not deserting her."

"My god." Her emerald eyes brightened. "She's even luckier than I thought she already was to have a guy like you."

"She's the prize, not me."

A WEEK LATER, DIANA accompanied Milan on his yacht for their sixth date. The sail under the starlit ocean emulated how Diana felt since meeting him.

Rocky. Unpredictable. Fast. Scary. Exciting.

Milan leaned on her from behind, his breath caressing her ear. "Are you cold? Here." He took off his Brunello Cucinelli blazer and hung it around her shoulders, his spicy cologne drenching the lapels.

The luxurious interior of his jacket felt like tiny hands massaging her shoulders.

He stood behind her again, pulled her close and rested his chin on her shoulder. "This is moving kinda fast. Six dates in about a week?"

"Yeah."

"Yet when we're together I get the feeling someone else is on your mind."

"Are you kidding?" She wrapped his jacket tighter around her. "I'm on a gazillion dollar yacht in the ocean sipping Armand de Brignac Brut Gold and wearing a Cucinelli blazer." She laughed. "What else could be on my mind?"

He turned her around, held her chin and brought his moist mouth in for a kiss.

She dropped her head and he let her go while sucking his lip.

"What are we having for dinner again?" She smelled fish but couldn't tell if it was from the kitchen or the ocean.

"Halibut and Balsamic blackberry sauce."

"Maybe we should go to the dining room."

He held her in place, looking down at her with half-moon eyes. "It's not ready yet."

She shivered.

"You're nervous."

"I keep thinking about what you said when we first met. You don't trust me. Has that changed?"

"No." He held her waist. "But I like you."

"What do you expect to come from this? You admitted this is a game."

"A game you started, Anna." He caressed her cheek and the hairs on her arms stood. "How we got to this moment doesn't matter. I'm attracted to you. I might be crazy, but maybe this could be something."

"You know that in a week?"

"I fell in love with Celestina in a day."

"I believe love takes longer to grow."

He pushed her blowing hair behind her ears. "Not always."

"Gray said you have women all over the world."

"Gray wants you for himself." He tangled his fingers in her crinkles. "He'd say anything."

"You said it too." She snuggled in the blazer.

"There's no one else, Anna."

"How can I believe that? Prove to me you think I'm special. Or is this just another part of the game?"

"All right." He kissed her hand. "Come with me."

CHAPTER FOURTEEN

If Heaven were on earth, it would've been the master bedroom of the *Celestina*. It was one thing to see pictures of wealth but to experience it became more than Diana could handle.

Milan closed the handcrafted, art nouveau double doors, and stood in front of them signaling she wasn't leaving until he was damn good and ready.

"Am I your prisoner?"

"Depends." He sauntered to her with unbridled lust in his eyes. "You want to be?"

She laid his blazer on the circular, king-sized bed.

With an erotic smirk, Milan got a slender box from the vintage nightstand. "I bought this for Celestina before she died. I swore I'd never take it out unless I met someone worthy of wearing it." He gave it to her. "Open it."

Diana stared at the velvet black box. "Milan—"

"Open it."

She untied the satin ribbon and lifted the lid to a stunning, white gold necklace.

"Oh, my god."

He took it, turned her around and fastened it around her neck. "It looks amazing on you."

"I can't accept this."

"I want you in my life, Anna." His hands followed the curve of her hips. "I don't care about how long it will last. I just want to enjoy having you in my arms and knowing you belong there." He turned her around and stood nose-to-nose with her. "I haven't felt this way since Celestina died."

"I'm not Celestina," she whispered against his lips. "I'll never be her."

"I want *you*, Anna." He seized her waist, slamming his flexible lips over hers.

"Mm." She wanted to pull away but her body ignored what made sense, and she gripped his shoulders, manipulating his movements for a deeper kiss.

He unlatched her lips one at a time, kept his eyes closed for a moment and then looked at her.

"You never said you wanted me." He rubbed his erection against her, her vulva growing wet. "Now I know you do. Your heart beats so fast when I'm close to you."

"Please." Her nipples swelled against the lace of her bra. "Please, don't do this."

"I won't make it easy for you to walk away." He slipped his hands underneath her dress, fondling her buttocks. "You're scared because this isn't neat or nice."

"You're right." She breathed hard, her pussy begging for another kiss. "I can't be a part of this life you have. Not in a million years."

"Do you want to be?" He eased the tips of his fingers inside her panties.

"Don't." She pushed his arm away. "How can I be with a man who doesn't trust me or better yet who I don't trust? There are things you'd never be able to share and I'm not okay with that."

"I don't want you involved in what I do." He straightened his posture. "I don't want another person I love getting hurt because of me. I'll shield you from the ugliness, Anna."

"But the ugliness is a part of you, Milan. We can't pretend it doesn't exist. You want two lives. One with me and the other focusing on your business. We can't separate them."

"Yes, we can." He squeezed her face and kissed her. "All that matters is how we feel about each other. Tell me another man's made you feel the way I do." He manhandled her thighs, her labia screaming for her to let him inside. "That anyone else makes you hot the way I do." His rough kisses left her lips numb. "You can't, can you?"

"You got to let me in all the way." She pinched the silver buttons on his white shirt. "I need to know everything about you."

"I can't do that." He kissed her, slobbering. "I won't put you in that danger."

She gripped his pecs through the linen material. "I'm in danger just by being with you."

"That's not true. I would do anything to protect you." His fingers pinched her sides. "I want you right here."

"I can't." She touched his mouth and turned when he tried to kiss her again. "I'm not ready."

"Bullshit." Wrinkles shot out across his forehead. "You get wetter every time I kiss you."

She touched his hand as he grabbed at her breast. "Listen—"

"Listen to your desires and the fire that's burning inside of you." He lifted her dress and shoved his hand into her bra.

"No." She wobbled, knees weak. "Milan, I can't." She pushed at him but all she wanted was to be in that bed, rocking against his naked body in the same rhythmic, magnetic way the boat swayed in the ocean.

"Anna." He sucked her cheek. "I'm used to getting what I want. Why should you be any different?"

"Please." She pushed at his hands as they roamed her body while the skirt of her dress went in all directions. "You're making this so hard."

"Good. I want you to give in."

"Stop."

He let go. "You don't get it. I'm in love with you already."

She fixed her dress. "You can't be serious."

"I am. Fuck how long we've known each other. I know what's in my heart and what's in my soul."

"I want to go back to my hotel now." She tried to pass, and he grabbed her.

"You could have a life you've only dreamed of. You'd travel to the most exotic places, shop in the most expensive boutiques, have more cars, money, servants and jewels than you could imagine."

"Let me go."

"Listen, damn it. You'd have the world at your beck and call. You'd provide the orders and watch them carried out before your eyes. I want to give you the life you deserve!"

"It's not about what you can give me but what you are!" She tugged until he let her arm go. "You can't just gloss over what you do. You can't expect me to forget that and just let you into my life!"

"I'm already in your life."

"Please." She wobbled, gripping her head. "I want to go back to my hotel."

"Anna."

"Please." She closed her eyes. "Take me back right now."

"Fine, but I never give up when I want something." He opened the doors. "I won't start now."

CHAPTER FIFTEEN

W hen Diana returned from her date with Milan she found Eric on the beach behind the hotel staring into the swirling bluish-green waves of the ocean.

During the day, hotel guests crowded the beach, but at night it resembled an isolated island apart from the rest of the world.

Diana rested beside Eric, not caring that her dress would be full of sand.

"You're gonna mess up your dress." Eric propped his wrists on his knees, the salty breeze tickling his hair. "Gray came by the hotel."

"What?"

"Yeah, he was looking for you and when I told him you were out with Milan, he looked like he wanted to strangle somebody."

"What is with him?" She tucked her leg underneath her. "I had three voice messages from him on my phone tonight. Why won't he leave me alone?"

"Because he likes you. Di, you can't just lead a man on and expect his feelings to go away."

"I didn't lead him on." She folded her arms. "I was upfront with him from the beginning and told him I only wanted his help."

"You were flirting with him to get what you wanted. How was your date with Milan?"

"I wish you wouldn't call it that."

"What should I call it?" He smacked his lips. "Bet you have him wound around your little finger—"

"I can't take this attitude anymore, Eric."

"You're so selfish, Di."

"Selfish?" Grit and sand covered the inside of her toes. "I'm trying to save my father's life. I'm not here on vacation, Eric."

"Seems like you need a reminder of that."

"I don't need this shit." She jumped to her feet and brushed off the back of her dress. "Good night."

"Just admit you're in over your head." He wiggled his toes in the sand. "Like I said you'd be."

"Okay, I am." She spread out her arms. "Guess I thought I had Milan figured out and I don't. There's no rulebook to this, but I'm doing my best."

"How long are you playing this game? What if it takes months or years to get answers?"

She stiffened. "So be it."

"Meanwhile George is probably in Hawaii somewhere sipping a Mai Tai, not giving a shit what happens to his daughter."

"Maybe he is." She pushed her toes into the sand. "Milan says he's in love with me."

Eric grinned, shaking his head.

"It can't be true, can it?" She sat again.

"Do you want it to be?"

The ocean waves wrestled in the moonlight as vibrant red streaks formed in the water.

"A part of me does."

Eric's nostrils flared. "And the other part?"

"The other part can't stop thinking about *you*."

He looked at her, grabbing more sand.

"I appreciate you so much, Eric." She touched his fuzzy arm. "No matter how much I push you away and how hurt you get, you're always there when I need you."

"Forget appreciation. I came to Miami hoping it would bring you back to me. It's killing me if that doesn't happen." He stretched out a leg. "I need clarity. After this is over, however long it takes, can we be together again?"

A lesbian couple walked along the shore holding hands.

"Give me something, Di. Please. A sign, anything. I love you so much. It kills me when you're off with Milan because he's getting to you." He touched her cheek. "I won't let him steal you from me. I don't care how rich, powerful or dangerous he is. He's not having you."

"Course not." She moved his hand. "He's trying to manipulate me and I won't let him."

"Are you trying to convince me or yourself?"

She sighed, leaning her head to the side. "Think we can trust Pam to stay quiet about who I am?"

"I don't know." He did a lazy shrug. "I don't really give a damn at the moment. We're talking about us now."

"No." She rubbed her temples. "This is about George and we gotta remember that."

"Not for me." He huffed. "I came to keep you safe and win you back. Are you any closer to finding out why Milan's looking for him?"

"I'm trying. I can't just ask the man why he's looking for George when I'm not supposed to even know who George is."

"What's the plan?" An accusatory glint shined in his eyes. "To keep seducing him so he'll tell you all his secrets? I doubt that will happen."

"You make me feel cheap when you say that."

"That's what you're doing." He scratched his shoulder. "How far are you gonna go?"

"Excuse me?" She stuck out her neck. "I don't like what you're implying."

"Would you sleep with him to get to the truth, Di? Because right now I'm not so sure."

"Fuck you, Eric." She stood. "It's easy to sit there and judge when you're not in my shoes."

"He'll kill you, Di." He stood, pulling up his dark-blue trunks. "Milan Vitale will kill you without a thought if he knew who you were."

"I know that!"

The female couple glanced toward them.

Diana whispered, "I have no choice in this."

"Stop dancing around and get some answers."

"I'm trying."

"Really? Because it looks like you're taking your time enjoying the good life." He stomped past her. "I hope you got a damn good plan for both our sakes."

"I'M SORRY, MISS PEACOCK." Milan's security guard blocked her from entering the gate a few days later. "You're not welcome here anymore."

She snatched off her shades. "I need to speak to Milan."

"I'm sorry. He's given the orders—"

"Let her in." Douglas walked through the corridor.

The guard nodded and opened the gate.

Douglas pulled her to him. "Hey."

Pam waited until the guard left and collapsed into Douglas' arms. "Everything's falling apart."

"Sh." He patted her hair, his furry dreads tickling her face. "What's wrong?" He escorted her to the chairs by the trees for privacy. "You're freaking out."

"I'm about to bust because I know all this shit will come down on me."

"I told you I'll protect you."

"Great job you're doing now, Douglas."

"I'd never have put you in this position if you'd be hurt. That's the last thing I want to happen."

"I need to speak to Milan." She put on her shades. "I don't wanna do this I want out."

"It's not that simple."

"*Make* it, simple. You got me into all this and now I'm losing everything. He fired me from the club. I refused again to sleep with Delgado, and Milan didn't like it. Douglas, I loved singing at the club."

"I'm sorry, but in the scheme of things, that's not the most important thing, Pam."

"Your operation is what's important and to hell with my life, right?"

"You knew things would change when you agreed to help me."

"I didn't agree," she shouted. "I did not agree, I fell in love with you like an idiot so I wanted to help you."

"You're doing it because it's right." Douglas sat, stretching out his long legs. "You're a good woman, Pam. Much better person than any of them could ever be."

"You're the fed, not me."

He sighed.

"You've been trained for this shit. You said you'd protect me and I don't think you can."

"I will." He hugged her. "I promise I won't let them hurt you."

"What if they find out you're the leak?" she asked against his stone-wall pecs. "We're dead."

"They won't know."

"You can't be sure of that." She sobbed. "You can't."

"Listen." He held her face. "I'll walk away from this investigation before I let anything happen to you."

"This is your assignment. You can't just walk away, and the FBI would kick you out or whatever the hell they do if an agent screws up a case."

"You mean more to me than any investigation." He wrapped his thick, fleshy lips over hers, killing her fears for at least a moment. "Milan had you fired from the club so move on. You don't need that job. I'll take care of you."

"Money's not the point. Singing is my dream, not a job. The Strawberry Lounge is the closet I'll get to entertaining. I love people hearing me sing. I crave it."

"You are too good for Milan and his sleazy club."

She swayed in her high-heeled sandals. "It was all I had."

"You have me." He kissed her. "You'll always have me, Pam."

CHAPTER SIXTEEN

"Pam?" Ramon gestured to her from the corridor with a cigarette hanging out his mouth.

Douglas squeezed his knuckles. "*This* motherfucker."

"Keep cool."

"Pam!" Ramon stomped toward them.

"I can't take his shit right now." Douglas marched past Ramon and the two exchanged furious glares.

"Yeah, your ass better leave," Ramon muttered to Douglas and yanked the cigarette out his mouth when he reached Pam. "What's that shit? I tell you, you're pushing me, woman."

"And if I continue to push, what'll happen?" She held her hips. "You'll hit me again?"

"Walk with me for a second."

She jerked away from him when he tried to grab her hand.

"Come on, girl." He pulled her to the walkway, his leather loafers squeaking against the tile. "I said I was sorry."

"Sorry?" She touched her tender jaw. "You slapped me last night, Ramon. And it wasn't the first time."

He hooked his fingers around his belt, the little cross earring dangling from his right ear.

"You're always talking about God but look at the shit you do."

He smoked. "You're perfect now?"

"Why do I put up with this shit?"

81

"Because you like the life." He flicked ashes in the air. "You're just like we all are, Pam. You want money and power like the rest of us. Besides..." He snickered. "You're addicted to me."

"Please. No one could adore you as much as you adore yourself."

He laughed.

"You didn't even stick up for me when Milan fired me, did you?"

"I sure as hell did." He grimaced. "I hate another man touching you, but didn't you say you owed Milan?"

She groaned. "Are you asking me to fuck Delgado for this deal?"

He threw his arm out and she stopped walking. "I'm telling you to do your part. Milan's done a lot for you, Pam. He took you from the slums and put you in the lap of luxury. Show some gratitude."

She scoffed. "And here he is, the real Ramon. It's always business with you, isn't it?"

"You damn right because you see this shit, Pam?" He pointed to the estate, sweat mixing with that gunk he wore in his hair. "This will be mine one day. When Milan's gone—"

"*If* Milan's gone." She stared at him. "Isn't that what you meant?"

He wiggled his shoulders, taking a drag. "Yeah. But the point is this might belong to me and I want the organization in a strong place if I become leader."

They continued walking.

"What would that make you if I owned all this?" He nudged her. "My queen, Pam. We could get married."

"Ugh." She scowled. "No thanks."

"Girl, you'll be begging me for a ring once I'm the master. It'll be you and me on the throne of the Vitale Empire." He slapped his hands, laughing. "Baby we'd own the world."

"Don't you already?"

"No." He twisted his lips. "We won't have to answer to nobody ever again because we'll be in charge. Money and power, baby. In this world that's all that matters."

"I love Douglas, and I always have."

"You can love who you want as long as you're fucking *me*."

"He's a better man than you'll ever be."

Ramon blew smoke in her face and she fanned. "He's nothing but some uppity nigger—"

"Shut up!" She stuck her finger in his face. "Don't you dare say that disgusting word in my presence. On top of all the other shit, you're a racist too?"

"I ain't racist." He spit, chuckling. "Douglas could be red, green, pink, white, I still wouldn't like his ass. He doesn't show me no respect."

"God, you disgust me." She walked faster, her heels scraping against the pavement. "We're over."

He caught up with her. "Too bad you don't call the shots in this relationship. You're my woman until I say otherwise."

"Oh, no I'm not." She swung her arm as she walked. "I can't stand to be in the same room with you anymore."

He grabbed her neck and pulled her to him.

"Ow!" She pushed at his chest.

"You're mine." He licked her ear. "I told you, Pamela. Stop pushing me. You're pissing me off and you know what happens when someone pisses me off."

"Let me go!"

"Shut up." He held her still. "Be a good girl and tell Milan you'll give Delgado the fuck of his life."

"Fuck you." She pushed him off and massaged her neck. "You don't own me, Ramon."

"This whole organization owns you. Bought and paid for."

He thrust his musty arms around her and kissed her.

She flinched, struggling not to vomit.

He smirked as if he enjoyed it more when she fought. "Keep that pussy warm for me until tonight."

He slapped her ass as he walked away.

GRAY APPROACHED THE intruder sleeping beside his pool and laid the tip of his gun on the man's forehead.

"Whoa!" George Wayans tumbled out of the chair, athleticism still present in his 57-year-old body. "What the fuck is wrong with you, man? Put that thing away!"

"I should shoot you for being dumb enough to come here." Gray lowered the gun. "You got *any* sense, George? For someone who's supposed to be so damn smart you sure do stupid-ass things."

George stretched his six-foot body in the chair, his striking hazel eyes melting into his light-brown skin. "We need to talk."

Gray jammed the gun into his pants, glancing around to see if anyone besides the servants lurked. "Ever heard of a phone?"

"We need to talk in person."

"What the fuck are you doing still in Miami? If Milan finds you—"

"I'm tired of running from my problems." George lay his head back and stroked his extended black goatee. "I've done that my whole life and it's why things are so fucked up. Been thinking about my kid lately."

"Oh, God." Gray exhaled. "So you're risking everything for a daughter who can't even stand you?"

"You'll never understand the guilt because you don't have kids. Not being there for Diana is my biggest regret, man. My biggest."

"Milan's trying to *kill* you, George."

"I wanna talk about your boy not Milan." Except for the wrinkles around George's neck he looked almost 20 years younger as if someone used make-up to age him. "He's not fooling me."

"What are you talking about?"

"He's behind Milan wanting me dead. It wasn't hard to figure out."

"You're nuts. Ramon wouldn't do that to you."

"Gray, you cannot be this naïve. He doesn't give a damn about us."

"I've known him longer than you and he wouldn't turn on us. He needs us."

George stroked the back of his edge up high fade, wiggling his sneaky eyebrows. "Maybe he needed us before but now we're in his way."

"You're wrong." Gray sat on the chaise lounge that mirrored the one George laid in. "Ramon's protecting you from Milan."

"Nah, Ramon loves keeping folks guessing." George stretched. "It would be the perfect plan to have me believe he's protecting me when all he's doing is fattening me up for the kill."

"Stop it. We're all in this together. You're the one turning on people."

"Never." He focused his intense stare on Gray. "I might not be worth shit in other ways but I always keep my word."

"Yeah, all right, George." Gray walked to the liquor cabinet. "You're driving me to drink."

"Why so jittery, Gray? Paranoid?"

He poured a glass of whiskey and slurped. "So much shit going on it's hard to stay afloat. You're wrong about Ramon." He rejoined George and sat. "Just get that out your head now."

"Uh-uh. He set me up with Milan, and he won't get away with it."

"You're innocent now? Lord knows you've done plenty of dirt."

"Yeah, but I own up to what I do." He shook his feet in black combat boots.

"You run from what you do, George. You have your whole life."

"Well." The arrogance abandoned his handsome face as if he were reflecting. "Never said I was perfect."

"How did we get in this?" Gray's knee pointed to the sky. "Because you, me and Ramon are exactly alike."

"Hell no." George pulled at his crew neck T-shirt. "That motherfucker is on another level. Straight crazy. He'd kill his own mother if it got him what he wanted."

"We're the same." Gray sighed, regretting that fact. "We all end up in a dick measuring contest every time we're in the room because we're too busy trying to be men instead of acting like one." He peeked into his whiskey before another gulp. "Anyway, Ramon didn't force us into this. But if you want out, then tell him." Gray snickered. "Let's see how lovely that turns out."

"I didn't say I wanted out but we're supposed to have each other's backs and if we can't trust each other how the hell is this gonna work?"

"We *can* trust each other." Gray finished his drink and slammed the square glass on the slate-colored concrete. "Shit we have no choice but to. It's how you play the game."

"I'm sick of playing the game." George stood, his fitted jeans making Gray jealous because his huge package was so hard to ignore. "My whole damn life I've played it and what do I have to show for it? Milan and Ramon's always talking about being a team and honor but it's all bullshit, Gray. Don't you get it? No one in this organization can be trusted. They use men like you and me to do their dirty work then throw us to the wolves. At least Milan keeps his word but Ramon..." He punched his palm, reminding Gray he was left-handed. "He'd kill *himself* to get the upper hand. Ramon is evil."

"He needs us as much as we need him to pull this off and he'd be a fool to turn on us."

"We're just pawns in his revenge fantasy."

"Enough." Gray stood, grabbing George's shoulders. "Trust me when I say everything's cool."

"Fine, I'm out of here." George strutted to the side entrance of the gate. "But don't say I didn't warn you."

"Where are you going?"

"Don't worry about it." George opened the metal gate, glaring at Gray over his shoulder. "I hope I can trust you, Gray."

"You can trust Ramon too. You're wrong about him. He knows it's not wise to turn on us so he won't."

George scoffed as he walked out the gate.

CHAPTER SEVENTEEN

"Fuck," Ramon whispered as Douglas came up to him outside Milan's study. "Get out my face."

Douglas shoved him into the study and pushed him on the rug.

"What the fuck?" Ramon scrambled to stand. "Don't put your hands on me again."

"Motherfucker." Douglas grabbed him in a headlock.

"Hey!" Ramon punched and clawed. "Get the fuck off me, asshole! What the hell is your problem, you black bastard?"

Douglas squeezed Ramon's neck, crushing his oxygen. "You're my problem."

"Get..." Ramon coughed and drooled. "Douglas, I can't breathe. I can't breathe, man!"

"Good." Douglas squeezed harder. "Because I need you to get the point. If you ever, *ever* lay a finger on Pam again I'll kill your bitch ass." He let him go, shoving him.

"Woo, man." Ramon laughed on all-fours, his neck throbbing. "You've fucked up now, Douglas." He punched the floor. "You've fucked up now, big boy."

"I'm serious." Douglas balled fists. "Go near her again and next time I grab your ass I won't let go."

Ramon massaged his throbbing neck. "You better hope nothing happens to Milan and I become leader because if so, you'd be dead before his body's cold."

Douglas pounced on Ramon, seizing his neck again. "Stay away from her. Touch her again and see what happens."

"Douglas!" Ivan leaped on his back. "Get off him. Stop it!"

Ramon broke free and socked Douglas in the nose.

"Ah!" Douglas stooped over, holding his face. "I'll kill you."

"Come on then!" Ramon bounced, throwing up fists. "I'm ready, fucker."

"Stop it." Ivan jumped between them. "Stop!"

"Kill your ass!" Douglas rammed into Ivan who almost fell over trying to keep the big man off Ramon. "You ain't shit, Ramon! You sure as hell ain't no man." Douglas sprayed spit. "You have no honor, no loyalty, no heart—"

"Shut the fuck up, faggot!"

"Faggot?" Douglas shrieked, ramming his chest into Ivan whose screams got no one's attention. "Say it again!"

"Faggot," Ramon snarled over Ivan's shoulder. "Kick the shit out of you."

"Yeah, do it!" Fire shot from Douglas' eyes. "Do it then."

"Douglas." Ivan held him back with both hands. "Listen—"

"Do it," he screamed. "Go on do it! Do it, Ramon! You bad. Do it!"

"Fuck it." Ramon shoved Ivan away and stood by the bookshelf, panting. "Your ass ain't worth it."

"Look at you." Douglas pointed over Ivan's shoulder. "Nothing but a coward."

"What the hell is this about?" Ivan yelled.

Ramon caught his breath and straightened his collar. "He's jealous of me as always."

"This isn't about no jealousy." Douglas let out an eerie cackle. "Just wait. I got something for your ass, Ramon. One day it'll be just you and me. No one to break us apart and I'm gonna tear your ass up."

Ramon blew him a kiss. "You promise?"

Ivan glared at him. "That's not helping."

Douglas charged Ramon again, and Ivan held him off this time. "What did Ramon do that got you wanting to kill him?"

"Besides just existing? He roughed up Pam."

Ivan looked at Ramon. "What?"

"I saw his bitch ass grab her in the yard."

Ivan held his waist. "Why did you do that?"

"We're a couple." Ramon huffed. "What we do is nobody's business."

"Pam is my business," Douglas warned. "You're paying for this."

"You and what army's gonna make me?"

Douglas went for him again.

"Enough!" Ivan held Douglas by the shirt. "We got more important things to worry about than this stupid feud."

"Throw his big ass out of here."

"Cool it, Ramon," Ivan said. "You don't run things yet and if it were up to me, you never would."

"I *will* run this shit and you both will answer to *me*."

"Convenient about Luca." Douglas blew out his cheeks. "How he just died suddenly?"

Ivan looked at Ramon.

"The man had been dying for years. You trying to say something, Douglas?"

"The only person standing in your way is Milan and when he's gone you get everything. The empire, the money, all of it."

"You better not be accusing me of something." Ramon gritted his teeth. "Better think long and hard before you go there, Douglas."

"You're burning too many bridges, man," Ivan told Ramon. "I only hope you burn along with them."

Ramon coughed and spit into the trashcan. "Suck my dick. When I'm leader I'll throw your ass out too."

"This is my family." Ivan stood chest-to-chest with Ramon. "You ain't throwing me out of nothing."

"Family, huh?" Ramon grinned. "Yet not family enough for them to leave all this in your hands? That's what kills you isn't it, Ivan? That even though you were Luca's blood kin he gave more

of a damn about me than he ever did of you."

"You!" Ivan grabbed him, raising a fist.

"Hit me." Ramon laughed. "I love making you idiots crazy and one day how you treated me will come back to haunt both your asses."

Ivan groaned, letting him go. "As I said, you ain't worth it. Let's go, Douglas."

"Yeah, I ain't worth it?" Ramon hollered as they left, his phone buzzing in his pocket. "That's not what your momma said." He answered his phone, "What?"

"You okay?" Gray asked. "Sound out of breath."

"It's just Douglas getting in my ass again. What is it?"

"Guess who just came to see me?"

"Queen Elizabeth? How the fuck should I know?"

"George."

Ramon smirked as he got his cigarettes out his pocket.

TWO WEEKS LATER

Milan laid bouquets on top of his parents' graves in the Vitale family cemetery.

He prayed for what seemed like an eternity and then brushed grass and leaves off the tombstones.

"My biggest fear is losing my mother," Diana said. "I couldn't imagine how I'd make it without her."

Milan sat on one knee resting his fist against his mouth. "What's her name?"

"Beverly," she said it too fast, so she didn't have time to make up a name in case Milan had heard of her mother.

"Did she raise you alone?"

"Yes." Diana thought about the many times George would take off during he and her mother's marriage. All the nights her mother worried to death wondering if he'd come home.

"I opened up old wounds?" Milan asked.

She batted away tears. "I'm fine."

"What about your dad? Did you know him?"

"Yes and no. You're lucky to have had such a close relationship with your father." Diana approached Luca's grave. "I'd have died to have that kind of connection with mine."

Milan pulled his lip. "My father taught me loyalty is the most important thing next to love." He smiled at her. "Do you agree?"

"Sometimes it's hard to stay loyal."

"Not if you love someone." He stood, pulling at his black slacks. "Did you enjoy the symphony last night?"

"Yes." She gushed, bringing her hands to her chest. "I didn't want to leave."

"Me either. I haven't felt this way about anyone since Celestina."

"She was killed because of you, wasn't she? That's why you didn't want me to know how she died." She squeezed his hand. "You didn't want to scare me off."

"Yes." He closed his eyes and exhaled. "We don't know who did it but I'm convinced one of my enemies took revenge against me through her."

"I'm so sorry."

"It meant the world that you came here with me today." He took her hand. "You've put everything in perspective."

She smiled.

"I don't want this life anymore, Anna."

"What are you talking about?"

He fidgeted as if to shake off what he'd said. "I'm having a party Saturday night for my closest loved ones. Will you come?" He wrapped his arms around her waist. "I have a big announcement to make about my

future."

She swallowed, glancing at the bodyguards who watched from the trees.

"This is very important, Anna." He kissed her. "Mr. Carter is more than welcome too. It's formal so you'll have to dress up. Will you come?"

"Yes." Her jumped as she wondered where the heck all this would lead. "I'll come."

CHAPTER EIGHTEEN

Diana snuck away from Milan's party and took in the fabulous art that filled the halls.

Every once in a while a guard would pop up, and she'd greet him with a smile while continuing her stroll.

She never let her guard down, knowing that any second they could realize who she was.

"Miss Hampton?"

Douglas' dreads always complimented his Nubian good looks but his buffed body stuffed in that regal tux created the dirtiest of thoughts.

"Is everything okay?" he asked.

"Yes, thank you." She touched the sides of her sequin, off-the-shoulder gown. "I needed a breather."

"Yeah uh, you looked like you'd faint in there."

She laughed. "I didn't expect him to make such a big deal out of me."

"Milan's crazy about you."

She smiled while the guests' laughter rang through the halls.

"He's invested in you." Douglas' expression hardened. "You realize how dangerous that is, right?"

She shook, her chandelier earrings dangling against her neck. "I told Milan I wanted to take it slow."

"That's not his way." He stood straight. "He wants what he wants when he wants it."

"Don't we all?"

"Watch your back. I wouldn't want anything to happen to you."

"Um, is there something you're trying to say, Douglas?"

His bowtie rose when he swallowed. "Enjoy your evening." He walked to the end of the hallway and ran up the spiral stairs.

When Diana turned back around, Eric came from around the corner looking classical-movie-star dapper in his white, slim fit tuxedo.

"You okay?" he asked.

"Milan can put on quite a show can't he?"

"Yeah he was introducing you like you're getting married or something." He examined her gold, floor length gown, his gaze stopping at her cleavage. "You look so beautiful, Diana."

"I know." She fidgeted, tucking her knee back into the slit. "You've told me a million times."

"I can't help it." His chest heaved as he took a deep breath. "Even in my fantasizes you've never looked this amazing. It's

impossible not to grab you and kiss you. You're so sexy—"

"Don't."

He pressed his lips together, eyes bulging. "When this is over, I'm the one who'll be there for you, not Milan. He only cares about Anna. He'd hate you if he finds out the truth."

She scratched underneath her tight bun. "I have it under control."

"We can't stay here forever."

"You don't have to be here, Eric. You can go back to Atlanta any time you want."

"Thought you weren't comfortable accepting that necklace." His nostrils flared. "Sure got comfortable quick."

"I didn't want to wear it." She touched Celestina's necklace. "But he insisted."

"He's ordering you around now?"

"Stop it."

"Stop what?"

"Being an asshole."

"How out of hand are you letting things get between you and Milan?"

"I'm *handling* it."

He parted his lips and pulled her to his puckered lips as if he wasn't even aware he was doing it.

"Eric." She pushed him away. "What the hell are you doing? There're cameras everywhere."

"I don't care. I wanna kiss you."

"If Milan thinks we got something going, it will ruin everything and I'll never find out the truth."

"Kiss me."

"No." She fought the urge to oblige him. "The cameras."

He grabbed her again. "Fuck the cameras."

"Eric." She shoved him away. "Stop. I mean it. You'll ruin everything."

Milan's butler came from around the corner. "Miss Hampton?"

Diana separated herself from Eric and put on a shaky smile. "Hello, there."

The slender, bald man smiled back. "Mr. Vitale's ready to make his big announcement and he wants you there."

She and Eric headed for the ballroom and broke off in different directions when they got there.

"Here she is!" Milan kissed Diana and pulled her to the front of the guests. "Now it's time for my big announcement!"

The guests clapped and howled.

"Let me say that this is not an easy decision." He took off his tuxedo jacket and handed it to a servant. "But one I needed to make for the future of me and this gorgeous woman right next to me."

"Ah," the audience swooned.

Diana twitched, wishing she was anywhere else in the world.

"A lot has changed for me." Milan waved his champagne glass. "But it's allowed me to put things into perspective. This decision will shock you, but it's something I've wanted to do for a few years now." He held Diana by her waist. "Thank you all for years of appreciation and support. Not only for me but for my father and the Vitale organization."

The guests cheered and whistled.

Milan did a deep sigh as he stared into Diana's eyes. "God's given me a gift, and she's standing right next to me."

The audience swooned again.

"Milan." Diana turned from everyone.

"She's being coy, but she knows how much I care about her." He kissed Diana's nose. "That grows each day."

Eric stood in the back of the room with agony etched on his face, and the pain in his eyes ripped Diana to pieces.

Milan beckoned to Ramon. "Ramon, come up here."

Ramon strutted past the people in a gaudy, red, velvet suit.

Milan grabbed him when he approached and slapped his arm around Ramon's shoulders. "You've always been my brother. Blood doesn't matter."

Ramon smirked, touching the cigarette behind his ear.

"Come on with this announcement," a woman yelled.

"Okay, okay!" Milan laughed. "The time has come. Everyone, I'm stepping down as the head of the Vitale Empire."

"What?" Diana gaped.

Ramon parted his lips, color seeping from his face.

The guests stared at Milan with their mouths wide open.

Douglas stormed out the room and Ivan's entire body drooped as if he'd lost hope for anything.

And Eric...

The guests' groans grew into blistering demands for an explanation.

"Please, listen. This wasn't sudden," Milan spoke over the chaotic crowd. "I know it's shocking, but I don't want this life anymore."

The audience quieted down.

"I never wanted this life."

"What?" the people at the front whispered.

"If that's true then why did you step in as the leader?" a silver-haired man asked. "You can't quit."

"Yeah," a woman shouted. "This is your family's legacy and yours. Luca is turning over in his grave, Milan."

"Ungrateful," a man barked. "He wanted the best for you. Gave you the kingdom on a platter and you don't want it?"

"He ain't man enough to handle all this, pretty lady," Ramon whispered to Diana, ogling her cleavage. "You know what they say. Never send a boy to do a man's job. I'm a *man*." His stare fell further into her chest. "You can take that however you want, mama."

"Humph." She rolled her eyes.

He winked at her with a smug grin.

"Listen, everyone." Milan tossed his head in the air with pride though it was obvious the guests' reactions hurt him. "I don't want it, and I'm sick of pretending. I'm not happy." His eyes watered. "And, I wanna be." He smiled at Diana. "Forever."

Ivan slammed his glass of champagne on the banquet table and left.

"This is a happy occasion not a sad one," Milan shouted. "This is the right thing to do for me and the organization. Ramon will be leader and he'll be a damn good one."

Ramon smiled like a man with the world at his feet, because now it was.

"In time you'll understand," Milan assured the weary audience who shook hands and fists in protests. "It's done. I hope one day you can accept my decision."

"If Luca wasn't dead already, this would kill him," a bearded man in a fedora said.

"Maybe so." Milan sighed. "But it's what's best for me. I can't do any better than that."

"Thanks, man. I love you." Ramon hugged Milan and smacked his cheek. "You did the right thing." He passed Diana and took another lusty look at her dress before swaggering out the room.

"Why?" Diana asked Milan. "Why would you do this?"

"It wouldn't have happened if not for you." He looked like a man who'd been reborn. "I love you, Anna."

She stopped breathing for a second.

"Did you hear me, woman?" His eyebrows dipped in the center. "I said I love you. I'm walking away from the only life I've known for you." He lifted her chin. "Say you'll be mine forever."

"I...I can't do this." Her breathing quickened. "Milan, this is too much. It's took much!" She pushed him away and ran through the crowd.

"Anna, wait!"

She ran out the ballroom, catching the stares of Gray *and* Eric.

CHAPTER NINETEEN

Milan ignored Douglas and Ivan's protests as they all went into the parlor. "I don't want to hear it."

"Tough because you will." Ivan slammed the door. "What the fuck did you do?"

Douglas grabbed his waist. "Are you out of your damn mind?"

"I handed over the empire to Ramon. What does it look like I did?"

"This isn't you," Douglas said. "You don't make big decisions at the spur of the moment."

"I don't want to be the leader of the organization anymore." Milan straightened his bowtie in the mirror. "Case closed."

"The hell it is," Ivan said. "You handed every fucking thing over to Ramon like you were selling him a hat! How could you do this without consulting us first?"

"Get this straight," Milan faced them. "I don't have to explain my decisions to anyone. It isn't a surprise. You both knew Ramon would take over."

"Only if something happened to you," Douglas insisted. "We sure as hell didn't expect you to just hand over the damn thing."

He shrugged. "Don't like it then take it up with my father."

Douglas leaned his head back, scoffing.

"What about the promise you made to Uncle Luca?" Ivan asked. "He'd be devastated you're turning your back on something that meant so much to him."

"That's the point!" Milan clapped. "This meant something to him not me. I never signed up for this life. I went along with it because it was my duty but that's it. No more sitting around dreaming and writing fantasies in a notebook." He yanked his shirt. "I have money, an amazing home, and things any man would be happy to have yet I'm miserable." He held back tears. "I'm miserable and for what? Power? I don't get how people fight over it every day yet I can't *wait* to give it away."

"Is this about Anna?" Ivan asked.

"She's the reason but not the cause."

Douglas shook his head, falling on the suede futon.

"It's simple." Milan smiled. "I'm choosing love and happiness."

"Love?" Ivan charged him with balled fists. "You've known that woman for three weeks and you're giving up everything for her?"

"I love Anna."

Douglas guffawed, stroking his dreads.

"I don't care if it makes sense to you." Milan meandered to the window and moved the velvet curtain. "I lost two people that meant everything to me." He stared into the garden, the lights casting a golden sheen over the flowers. "I almost

never recovered from Celestina being killed. I vowed I'd protect her, but as long as I lead the empire, she was on borrowed time."

"You didn't pull the trigger on her, Milan," Ivan said. "You can't keep blaming yourself."

"I did pull the fuckin' trigger!" He turned from the window. "I pulled it when I brought her into this world. How dare I put someone I claimed to love in that position?"

"She knew what she was getting into," Ivan said.

"I swore I'd never let another woman I love be in danger because of me."

"Leaving the empire won't make Anna any safer," Douglas said. "You take the man out the mafia but you can't make the mafia forget he was there. You have enemies that will never go away. I don't care if you leave the country, you'll always be a marked man."

"No." Milan walked across the carpet, concentrating on his steps. "Anna and I can go away. We can disappear. I have the money to do that. I'll make sure no one will find us."

"Stop talking like this!" Ivan stomped his foot. "You cannot do this. You can't leave the empire to Ramon. There's too much shit going on."

"I'm not giving it to him *tonight*. There are legal matters to clear up. It'll take months to transfer things over, and I've got things to do before I'm done."

"Like what?" Douglas asked.

"George Wayans. I'm not leaving until his head's on a platter and I'm setting it on fire. There's the leak too. I'm not going to leave Vitale while this shit's going on."

"Does Anna love you?" Ivan asked. "If not you're throwing away everything for uncertainty."

"If she doesn't, she will." Milan slipped a yellow carnation from the bouquet of assorted flowers on his desk. "I'll make sure of it."

GRAY CAME DOWNSTAIRS as Ramon howled and twirled in the hallway. "You must be on cloud nine, huh?"

"Try cloud one hundred. Did you see that shit, Gray? He handed the empire to your boy. Ha, ha!" Ramon shook him. "Man, I didn't think it would be this easy."

"Congratulations." Gray groaned, tucking his hands in his pockets.

"You ain't happy for me? Awe." Ramon snickered. "You're jealous because you lost your girl?" He whistled. "She's looking delicious in that dress. Like sex on a stick."

"I'd given Anna everything."

"Milan's giving her more than she can handle." Ramon took the cigarette from behind his ear. "Bet he's tearing that pussy up."

"Shut up. She's not fucking him."

Ramon laughed, lighting his cigarette. "Whatever you say, Gray."

"You're wrong."

"The man walked away from his livelihood for her, Gray. She's gotta have some damn good pussy for a man to do that." He puffed smoke. "I bet she's tight. Nah." He wiggled his nose. "Too old to be tight. Maybe she squirts. I'd give up the empire too for a bitch that squirts."

"You're disgusting." Gray got in his face. "Don't talk about Anna like that."

"Oh, sorry." Ramon patted Gray's shoulder, grinning. "Didn't mean no disrespect but hey, gotta stop fooling yourself, Gray."

"Fuck!" Gray went to punch the antique mirrored cabinet.

"Hey!" Ramon grabbed him. "You break that and Milan will break your knees."

"I'm so sick of him. He has everything. Does he have to have Anna too?"

"Forget that slut." Ramon put his arms around Gray's shoulders. "Once Milan's out the way, we'll have everything we want. You'll be the shit for real."

"I want Anna."

"I told you she's a gold-digger like they all are. Did you see her?" Ramon yanked the cigarette out his mouth. "Milan was introducing her like she was the Queen of England and she loved every minute."

Gray's jaws pulsated. "I saw it."

"Once I'm the leader I'll get you all the pussy you want. Forget Anna. She has no respect for you. She thinks you're weak."

Gray trembled, sweat bursting through his forehead. "I'm not."

"Then show her that." Ramon poked Gray's chest. "I told you to stop letting these bitches run all over you. You're the man, right?"

"Yeah." Gray nodded, swaying. "I am the man. I can't let her get away with this."

"That's right." Ramon popped the cigarette in his mouth. "Handle your business."

"What do I do?"

"Teach that bitch that she can't run over you without paying the consequences." Ramon strutted up the stairs. "She's in the study."

CHAPTER TWENTY

Diana jerked up on the couch when Gray barged into the study. "Well, hello, Anna."

"What do you want?" She finished wiping her eyes and put her mirror back in her purse.

"What's this?" He slunk toward the leather couch with his chest out. "Crying?"

"Go away, please."

He took off his blazer and draped it on the back of the sofa.

"What are you doing?"

"Let me guess, your conscience weighing on you?"

"What the hell are you talking about?"

He leaned over the arm of the sofa, his face inches from hers. "I know I'm not worthy to be in your presence but if you can spare a few moments of your time I'd be forever grateful."

She stood. "Are you drunk?"

"No." His eyes caressed her curves. "Does teasing men get you off, Anna?"

"I don't have time for this."

He grabbed her before she got to the door. "Oh, you're not going anywhere yet."

"Let go of me or I'll scream, Gray."

His eyes narrowed. "Shut up."

"What?"

"I said shut up." He tugged on her arm. "You're listening to me now."

"Who the hell do you think you're talking to?"

"You tell me." He stared at her cleavage. "A slut? A whore? You tell me who I'm talking to."

"This is..." She tried to break free. "This isn't funny, Gray."

"I agree none of it is funny." His fingers left reddish marks on her skin. "It's not funny how you used me and threw me away. Not funny how you walk around like you own the place and you wouldn't even know Milan if it weren't for me."

"Let me go. You're hurting me."

"Am I?" He tugged harder. "You didn't care about hurting *me*."

"I was honest with you from the beginning."

"Not how I saw it." He pawed her. "You seduced me to get to Milan. That was your plan all along. Once again I was a fool."

She struggled. "Let me go!"

"Scream all you want." He turned her toward him, grabbing her other arm. "The ballroom is all the way across the house."

"Get away from me, Gray." She tried to reach for his face. "I mean it!"

"What's the next part of your plan?"

"There is no plan. You're crazy."

"Trying to finagle your way into Milan's money?"

She tried to shake herself free. "I don't want his money."

"You want *something*."

Diana squeezed her lips together to thwart his kisses. "Get away from me."

"I bet you laughed at how stupid you thought I was."

She grunted, tussling with him. "I can't help I don't feel the same as you do about me. This isn't you, Gray." She cringed deep within her bones. "You don't treat women like this."

"No, the wimp you tossed away isn't me." He breathed, veins pulsating in his face. "*This* is the real me, and I'm sick of being taken advantage of by sluts like you." He shoved her on the couch and got on top of her. "I'll show you why I'm the better man!"

"No." She swung her fists in his grip. "Damn it! Stop."

"You brought this on yourself, Anna." Gray kissed her cleavage, slobbering. "You can't keep doing what you do to men."

"Stop. Get off right now!"

"I love you, Anna." He soaked her in sloppy, humid kisses while pressing his hard middle against her. "I thought you were different, but all you care about is money and power."

"Gray." She grabbed her purse from underneath her.

"I'm getting what I'm owed tonight." Gray grabbed her breast.

"Stop!"

"Yes, Anna. You'll want me tonight. Right here, in Milan's house."

"No!" She slammed her knee in between his legs, and he howled as he fell to the floor.

Diana got her gun from her purse and aimed it at him. "Touch me again."

Gray wobbled to his feet, moaning.

"Touch me again." She sat up straight. "Go on. I want you to so I have an excuse to shoot your ass."

"Why..." He stumbled as he moved from the couch. "Why do you have a gun?"

"For assholes like you who can't take no for an answer." She eased off the couch. "You get the point now?"

"Yeah, yeah." He waved his shaking hands. "I'm sorry, okay? I didn't mean to—"

"I don't wanna see you again, Gray. Ever."

"I'm sorry."

"You're pathetic. You spend your time trying to prove you're a man when you don't know what being a real man is about."

He held his crotch, grunting. "Anna—"

"I felt sorry for you but after what you just pulled any ounce of pity I had for you is gone."

"I love you. I mean it. Just tell me what you want. Please."

"I don't want you and I never will."

He dropped his head, got his blazer, and left.

ERIC CAME OUT THE BATHROOM as Ramon and Gray came from around the corner. "Shit." He ducked behind a statue and the men stopped at the elevator.

"Why do I keep listening to you?" Gray huffed. "Now Anna hates me."

Ramon grinned. "Hey, I didn't tell you to attack the woman."

"Attack?" Eric whispered.

Ramon set his champagne glass on the banister and lit a cigarette. "Chill. You're about to live the life you always wanted, and that's because of me."

"I don't get you." Gray loosened his bowtie. "All you care about is running the empire. What about love?"

"Love don't pay the bills or keep you in the lap of luxury."

"You've said plenty of times you won't let anything get in your way, Ramon. How do I know that doesn't include me and you'll turn on me as fast as I can blink?"

"Really?" Ramon puffed. "And what do I have to do to convince you I'm loyal? Suck your dick? I'm giving you the fucking world.

What's more loyal than that? Shit, Gray, you're the best friend I've ever had."

Eric squinted.

"You're changing, man," Gray said. "You're obsessed with the money and the power."

"Lighten up." Ramon tapped Gray's chin. "Get that bitch Anna out your mind and concentrate on how great you'll have it from now on. We'll own the world."

"You just don't get it. Anna's special."

"She's *trouble*."

"I'm going home." Gray pulled his keys out his blazer pocket. "I've had enough of you and Milan for one night."

"Hey." Ramon gestured at Gray as he walked away. "Let me know if George pops up again."

After Ramon and Gray left, Eric emerged from behind the statue, smiling about the newfound information.

CHAPTER TWENTY-ONE

"Sure Milan didn't get suspicious that you left the party?" Pam sat Indian-style on her couch, eating spaghetti.

"I don't give a damn." Douglas threw his tuxedo jacket on the loveseat and sat in it. "It's been hard enough playing the role but now *Ramon's* gonna be in charge?" He released a defeated breath. "Maybe I should pull out."

"You can't do that. There's no one the FBI can put in there who can get as close to Milan as you have."

"Thought you wanted me out of this."

"Well, this isn't about me." She slurped pasta into her succulent mouth. "Justice is long overdue."

"I gotta nail their asses before Ramon becomes leader because the first thing he'll do is kick my black ass to the curb."

She smiled. "You look so handsome in your suit. Did you enjoy the party?"

"Hell no." He sat back, crossing his legs. "It makes me sick being around them. I couldn't leave fast enough."

She bit into her garlic bread, blushing. "I can't believe Milan's stepping down like this. I guess that proves how powerful love is. We should know."

He caught the spark in her eyes.

"Love threw you for a loop." She bounced, beaming. "You came here to do a job and fell in love with me without warning."

He guffawed, touching his mouth. "Yeah, okay."

"You deny it? You fell for me when Milan introduced us."

He studied her, remembering that day. "I'd never seen a woman as beautiful in my life."

"And I'd never seen a man as sexy and handsome."

"I wondered what the hell you saw in that douchebag Ramon."

"And I told you sometimes you gotta love the one you're with." She wrapped spaghetti around her fork. "I wanted you physically the second I saw you, but it was your heart, your kindness and tenderness that drew me in."

"I hated thinking about you and Ramon." He tapped the arm of the chair. "Him kissing you and touching you. It damn near killed me."

"I wanted you the whole time." She walked to him and sat on his lap. "I love your dreads." She rubbed them against her cheek. "I love the way they feel on my face. So soft." She sniffed them. "I want to be with you so much, Douglas."

He widened her robe and sucked her neck, his lips causing pink spots on her delicate skin. "You're so beautiful." He pulled the robe off her shoulders and kissed her snow-white cleavage. "Every day, every night you're all I think about." He slipped his hands under her buttocks and lifted her as he stood. "You're the only reason I'm doing this."

"We'll leave this all behind when it's over." She kissed him as he laid her on the couch and sucked her pink nipple. "It'll be like a bad dream." She moaned, shoving her fingers into his hair. "I can't wait until I can wake up in your arms without having to worry about Milan or the organization. Our love is bigger than his power, Douglas." She gripped his cheeks, pulling him inside her electric smile. "Not even Milan can stop what's in store for us."

"That's right." He pulled down her white, cotton panties and kissed his way to her sweet spot. "I love you, Pam." He propped her leg over his shoulder as she gyrated, her body begging for more. "I always will."

DIANA ESCAPED FROM Milan as he bid his party guests goodnight and met Eric in the garden.

Eric grunted, walking from behind a podium. "'Bout time."

"I couldn't get away from Milan. Hurry and say what you gotta tell me because he'll be looking for me."

"Malton attacked you?"

"I'm fine."

"Are you sure?" He touched her face. "What did he do? If he hurt one hair on your head—"

"It's okay, Eric." She patted her purse. "Got my gun, remember? Gray's got the point now."

"I could kill him." Eric's cheeks expanded. "He better be glad he left before I got a hold of him."

"What did you need to say?" She looked toward the corridor, the voices of the departing guests carrying through the night sky. "Is it about my dad?"

"I heard Gray and Ramon talking. Apparently George is in town and has seen Gray."

"What?" Diana grabbed his lapel. "So, Gray knows where my dad is?"

"Maybe."

"Why would my father reach out to Gray when Milan's trying to kill him? Isn't he afraid Gray would tell?"

"Ramon and Gray seem to be protecting him. Maybe hiding him from Milan."

"But, why?"

"That's what we need to find out." Eric checked his watch. "You ready to head back to the hotel?"

"Uh, no." She looked back. "Milan wants me to stay."

"That's not a good idea, Di."

"I can't keep making excuses when he wants to be alone with me. I'll do whatever it takes to get the info I need."

Eric glanced sideways. "What do you mean by 'whatever'?"

"Eric—"

"I asked you a question." He grabbed her, forcing her eyes on him. "What do you mean by 'whatever'?" He lightly chuckled. "Are you saying you'd sleep with this man to find out the truth?"

She turned her head and with his finger he turned it back toward him.

"Answer me. Are you going to sleep with Milan tonight?"

"No." She avoided eye contact.

"Look at me." He shook her until she did. "Are you going to sleep with him?"

"I don't plan to."

"What do you mean by that?" His top lip trembled. "Either you will or you won't."

"I don't *want* to."

He let her go, breathing hard through his nostrils. "You sure about that?"

"Goodnight, Eric." She turned and walked on the cement path.

"Di." He jumped in front of her. "You can't do this."

She quickened her pace, holding her dress on one side. "I didn't say I was."

"But you're attracted to him." He hurried beside her. "Admit it."

She stopped, her heels scraping the cement. "Don't do this."

"*You* don't do it," he yelled. "You *can't* sleep with that man."

"Sh. My father's life is in danger, Eric. I'll do anything to save someone I love."

"You'll hate yourself if you do this."

"If something happens to my father, and I didn't do everything to help him, I'll hate myself if I don't." She walked away.

"Di!"

She kept walking.

CHAPTER TWENTY-TWO

Gray downed another shot of whiskey beside his moonlit pool. Usually it calmed him but nothing put out the fire of the damage he did tonight.

"Fuck. I wish I never heard of Milan Vitale."

"Ain't that the truth?" George strolled toward the pool. "What's up?"

"Damn it, George." Gray shuddered, clenching his glass. "You scared the shit out of me. Stop sneaking around. How do you keep getting past the alarm?"

"Why you look like you just came from the Oscars?"

"Milan had a party, and we had to dress up." Gray ripped off his bowtie and tossed it aside. "What do you want?"

"First, tell me what's got you drinking whiskey like water." George stood by the liquor cabinet. "Stressed about what I told you about your boy Ramon?"

"Stop calling him *my* boy. We're all in this together."

"I always liked you, Gray." George blinked. "You're a little soft for my taste but a cool dude."

"I am *not* soft."

"Don't take offense." George flashed his palm. "It's a compliment. Means you got heart. You're just like me, searching for something bigger and better. I always saw you as a kindred spirit."

"You singing *Kumbaya* next? What do you want, George?"

"Why'd Milan have a party, anyway?" His face twisted. "It's not his birthday or anything."

"He announced he's quitting as the leader."

George's mouth opened.

"He has to settle the legal stuff before it becomes official."

"Are you kidding me? Why did he do that?"

"For a woman," Gray mumbled, shaking his foot. "A fascinating, beautiful woman with the most gorgeous hazel eyes." He stared at George. "Eyes just like yours."

"A woman?" George tugged on his earlobe. "Gotta be more reason than that."

"This woman is amazing." Gray stared into the water. "A woman I'd give up everything for too if I had it."

"Wow."

"He says he's wanted to leave all long but Anna Hampton showed him the way." Gray rolled his eyes. "The spectacle was pathetic. Milan standing up there like he's some king. Made me sick."

"Luca's doing somersaults in his grave." George sat on the leather bench with the embroidered trim. "You're in love with this Anna, aren't you?"

"It's funny. I'm getting so close to something I've always wanted but the closer I get I'm caring about it less and less."

"Welcome to the club. All my life I've been a shark trying to get that big meat and then when I can reach up and grab it, I wonder if I ever wanted it. Maybe for me it was the chase. But when I think of all that money and power, commonsense leaves, and I rely on my mental ammunition to get me back to where I should be."

"What's your mental ammunition?" Gray went to the liquor cabinet and filled his glass again.

George took out his phone, swiped the screen a few times and handed it to Gray. "*She's* my mental ammunition. The only thing that brings me back to reality if even for a short while."

Anna.

"Who is this?"

"Diana."

"What?" Gray shrieked, almost dropping the phone.

"Be careful, man. That phone wasn't cheap."

"This is your daughter?" Gray stabbed the screen with his fingertip. "This is Diana?"

"Yes. Why?"

Gray gaped, handing the phone back to George. "Never mind." He took two long gulps of whiskey.

"What's up?" George narrowed his eyes. "Something I should know?"

"No." Gray coughed as he sat.

"I did a great job of fucking things up with her." George put the phone away. "I wish I could turn back time and be the dad she deserves but it just ain't in me, you know?"

Gray sipped, barely paying attention.

George stood, fixing his pants. "Guess I'll be going."

"Wait, wait, wait." Gray reached for him. "Since you're here, have a drink."

"Maybe I shouldn't."

"You should." Gray grinned as he laid on the lounge chair with his arm tucked behind his head. "Let's chill like old times."

George sat again, squinting.

"Tell me more about your daughter." Gray rocked his head, smiling. "I bet she's a fascinating woman."

"MM." MILAN WRAPPED his arms around Diana as soon as she got into his deluxe bedroom of sparkling golden décor and crystal fixtures. His almond cologne sprinkling the air. "It was killing me." He breathed into her ear, wetting it. "Being so close, wanting to touch you and couldn't."

Her nipples perked up when his hand outlined her hip. "Milan."

He exhaled as if he'd been without air for days. "I've never wanted a woman so much." He kissed her neck and she moaned out of instinct. "You feel the same, Anna." His pushed his dick against her ass. "Your body's telling me how much you want this."

Her knees wobbled. "I can't stay long."

"Stay long." He unzipped the back of her dress and tugged at the latch of her satin bra. "Stay forever."

"No." She tensed, her body throbbing with a passion she hadn't experienced since breaking up with Eric.

"Stay with me, Anna."

"No." She laid her head back on his shoulder, writhing from the rhythm of his hips.

"Why?" He undid her bra and tickled her throbbing nipple. "You have nothing to run to except an empty hotel room." He licked inside her ear, her pussy dripping. "With an empty bed. Stay the night." He clutched her neck rougher as if to demand it. "*Stay*. For the rest of your life."

"No." She pushed him away, struggling to zip up her dress.

"You're going the wrong fuckin' direction." He grabbed her, forcing the zipper down again.

"No, stop." She tussled as he yanked it down, breaking it. "Milan! Look what you did."

"What the fuck is the *problem*?" He waved his hands in her face. "Why are you fighting this and what we could be?"

She tucked her hanging dress under her arms to shield her breasts. "I'm not ready for this. You misunderstood."

"You want me but every time I get close to you, you push me away."

She folded her arms but her dress refused to stay straight. "You tore my dress."

"I don't give a fuck. I proved my love for you tonight and you gotta give me something, Anna."

"Is that a threat? Because I don't care who you are, you're not making me do something I don't want to." She turned away from him and he held her.

"But, you want this. Anna, please." He laid his head against hers. "You don't have to be afraid anymore. That's why I'm stepping down. So you'll be safe."

"This life is a part of you no matter what you do or say."

"We can leave." He rubbed her arms. "We can disappear."

"No."

"Please." He touched her neck. "Anna, I love you. I've opened my heart to you. Please, don't turn your back on me. I have nothing else."

"Nothing else?" She laughed while he stood there looking pitiful. "You have everything. This isn't about love, Milan. This is about a spoiled brat who's used to getting everything he's ever wanted so he can't take it when someone says no to him."

Lines formed between his eyebrows.

"Properties in different countries, vacations all over the world." Diana gestured to him. "An estate bigger than Queen Elizabeth's, money pouring out of your ass and still that's not enough?"

"No."

"Why isn't it, Milan? Why isn't it enough?"

"Because none of this shit matters if I don't have you."

She stood back, panting. "You can't love me, Milan."

"I do." He closed his eyes. "I swear with every inch of me, I do." He dropped to his knees in front of her. "I was a shell of a man before you and you made me whole again."

She blinked back tears.

"You know I love you." He sniffed and kissed her hand. "Stay the night. We don't have to make love. Let me hold you." He stood and kissed her, diminishing her doubt. "Stay in this moment with me. Doesn't it feel good?"

She dropped her head, sniffling. "Yes and that's what scares me."

"You don't have to love me now. Just don't run away, Anna. Please." He held her tighter. "Don't run away."

"What scares me the most is you make me doubt myself." She moved from him. "And, I hate that. I don't even know myself anymore."

"That's love, Anna." He clenched her face. "You're in love with me and you can't keep fighting it." He drew in for a kiss when her phone beeped.

"I have a text," she whispered. "I have to get it."

Milan groaned, holding her face.

"Would you pass me my purse, please?"

He got it off the dresser decorated with patterned veneers, handed it to her and sat on the bed. "You could be making love to me on this bed." He stroked the patterned spread. "It's your choice."

Diana imagined the passionate scenario then came back to earth and read Gray's text.

We need to talk. Don't ignore me.

She glanced across the room at the armoire with the Honey Walnut finish.

Milan's forehead lowered. "Are you all right?"

She cleared her throat. "May I have some privacy?"

"Are you staying with me tonight?"

"Please. I need to make a call."

He stood with an accusatory glint in his eye, nodded and left the room.

Diana pushed the call button. "What the hell is your problem, Gray? You're sicker than I thought if you think I want anything to do with you after what you did tonight."

"The incident in the study—"

"*Incident*? You tried to rape me, Gray."

"I didn't try to rape you, Anna."

"Then what the hell would you call it?"

"Come to my place. We need to talk about something important."

"Are you insane? Like I'd go to your house after what you did."

"You don't have a choice. I can ruin everything for you."

Her heart beat faster.

"Aren't you curious to know why?"

She cursed under her breath. "If you're lying to get me back to your place—"

"You don't want me. You've made that loud and clear. I got the point."

"Finally." She stared at the cedar drawers of the huge chest. "No way am I coming to your place so you can attack me again."

"You have a gun, remember?" An ominous pitch livened his tone. "Trust me, you won't want to miss this conversation."

CHAPTER TWENTY-THREE

G ray's housekeeper showed Diana to the pool and left.

Gray stood from the aluminum table and chair set, smiling. "What took you so long?"

"I had to go back to the hotel and change." Diana patted the side of her jeans. "I have my gun."

He stopped in front of her, face beaming with arrogance as if he was the master of the universe. "Why did you have to change?"

"The zipper broke on my dress. Does it matter?"

"That dress looked so pretty on you." His tongue peeked through his teeth. "I was hoping I'd get one last chance to see you in it."

"Say what you're gonna say or I'm leaving."

"What you're wearing now..." He ogled her. "Is far from disappointing though."

She sighed, crossing her arms.

"You look even sexier in jeans and sneakers." He snickered. "I bet you tried to pick out an outfit that wouldn't turn me on. Didn't work."

"You're full of shit." She turned to leave.

"Hold on." He snatched her hand.

"Uh-uh." She flung her arm back. "Don't touch me again, Gray."

He backed away. "Don't leave."

"Then get to the point. I'm sick of these games."

"You're playing a bigger game than anyone." He got a glass and opened the liquor cabinet. "Aren't you, *Diana*?"

She froze.

"You are Diana Wayans, right?" He raised the whiskey bottle. "Sit and have a drink with me. I'll make you a cocktail. Something tells me you could use one."

Her breath caught in her throat.

"I found you fascinating before but even more now." He sat, sipping from his glass. "So you like cats? Had one when you were a kid, didn't you?"

She held her breath.

"You were a little jock in school too. You were on the basketball and track team in high school." He winked. "You keep in shape."

She charged him. "How the hell do you know this?"

"You're a smart one. Had us all fooled. All that stuff about loving art and culture—"

"I do love art and culture."

"But you didn't like spending time with me, right?"

She tried to control the shaking in her voice. "I'm guessing you plan on blackmail or something?"

He laughed. "Diana, darling. You have nothing I want." He licked his lips as his stare glided over her body. "Nothing monitorial if that's what you mean. I don't want to hurt you. I love you, Diana."

"Oh, jeez." She rolled her eyes. "First Milan and now you?"

"I still want you."

"Are you going to tell Milan who I am?"

"Diana, Diana." He threw back his shoulders. "If I did that you'd be wrapped in a garbage bag with a gunshot between your eyes before noon tomorrow. That's the last thing I want."

She tucked in her lips. "Then what do you want besides me?"

"I want to protect you." He exhaled, his face losing its cockiness. "I'm sorry about earlier. That wasn't me and if I could take it back, I would. But what I did wouldn't compare to what Milan would do if he found out who you are."

She moved closer to the chair. "*What* do you want?"

"I want you to stop seeing Milan."

"I'm not leaving until my father is safe. Tell Milan. He won't believe you over me, anyway."

"He would and he'd kill you without blinking. Go back to Atlanta before you get killed. Why not unless..." He twisted his mouth as if he'd vomit. "God, you haven't fallen for him have you?"

"No."

"You sure? Anyone who falls for Milan ends up the same way. Celestina thought she'd be different and now she's maggot food."

"I'm *not* falling for him."

"He said he loved you? Milan never says that if he doesn't mean it. Diana, you're playing with a fire you can't put out. I'm trying to save you."

"I can take care of myself."

"George was here tonight."

She blinked. "My father was here?"

"Mm-hmm."

"Jesus, Gray." She plopped on the chair beside him. "Where did he go? How long was he here?"

"He wasn't here but a few minutes, and I don't know where he went."

"Does he know I'm here?"

"No." Another shifty smile graced his face. "I didn't say a word."

"Why is Milan looking for him? Tell me."

He shrugged.

"Gray."

He smirked. "Can't help you there."

"You mean you won't and I can't understand why."

"It's best if you don't know."

"Damn you." Diana stood and stomped away from the chair. "How can I find him?"

"People don't find George he finds you."

"Is he coming back here?"

He drank and licked his lips. "Your guess is as good as mine."

"Please, don't tell Milan who I am."

"Man, you are beautiful when you beg."

"You want my forgiveness for what you did tonight? You owe me this, Gray."

She waited for an answer and when he gave none, she rolled her eyes and left.

MILAN HOPPED DOWNSTAIRS the following night and found Ramon waiting for him with a bewildered expression and a folder in his hand.

"We need to talk."

"Not now." Milan breezed past him and into the parlor. "Anna's coming over tonight—"

"Fuck, Anna." Ramon charged into the room and shut the door. "This is more important than Anna will ever be."

"I doubt that." Milan overlooked his hair in the oval mirror behind his desk. "Everything has to be perfect tonight concerning Anna."

"Anna this, Anna that."

"I'm marrying her."

"What?"

"She's the one, Ramon." Milan patted his hair, looking at Ramon through the mirror. "I lost Celestina. I won't lose Anna too."

"Losing Anna will be the last thing on your mind if you're in prison."

Milan turned. "What?"

Ramon shook the folder. "Sit down."

"What's that folder?"

"Pam and Douglas were here earlier." He grimaced, squeezing the folder. "Kissing and carrying on right in my face. She's making me look like a fool."

"Too bad, so sad." Milan sat. "Get to the point."

"While they were here I went to Pam's to do some investigating."

"And?"

"She's been acting weird for a while so I thought she was hiding something. I snooped around her place and I found this shit." He tossed the folder on Milan's desk.

Milan opened it. "What is this?"

"Papers and notes." Ramon scratched behind his earring. "Stuff about the organization, inside info about our deals and business."

Milan tore through the folder yanking out Pam's handwritten notes of detailed conversations along with their dates. "What the fuck? Did you tell her this stuff?"

"Fuck no. I'd never betray you, Milan."

"Sure you didn't spill these secrets in the heat of passion?"

"I'd never tell Pam about what we do." Ramon held his waist, eyebrows forming a scowl. "She's been watching us, listening and keeping records. There's only one explanation. Pam's the leak."

Milan panted, squeezing the papers. "That's impossible."

"It's right in front of you isn't it? We trusted her and she was the leak the whole damn time!"

"Hold on." Milan laughed. "You're saying Pamela is FBI?"

"No, but maybe the feds put the heat on her and made her an informant. Why would she have this stuff then? She's been sitting back and recording shit that can put us all in prison."

"Ah!" Milan threw the papers at him. "Then you must've fucked up."

"Me?"

"If you didn't tell her this information, then she must've heard you running your mouth, and I told you not to handle business matters in front of her."

"I didn't!" Ramon swayed, huffing and puffing. "She's been sneaking around you, me *and* Douglas. That's why she was fucking us. She was trying to get information."

"After all I've done for her? I plucked her from nothing. Gave her a job where she could make more money than she could dream of. Showed her the good life."

"Yeah, and she was a snake the whole time." Ramon cracked his knuckles. "The bitch's gotta go. It's her or us."

Milan rocked, rubbing his nose.

"We have to take her out."

"I want talk to her first." Milan stood. "We'll call her over tomorrow."

"Fuck talking. She's the leak! You expect her to admit it?"

"We won't let on we know. I'll throw out some things to see how she reacts."

"Why?" Ramon leaned to one side, holding his waist. "Fuck this wasting time shit. I can take her out myself tonight."

"No." Milan raised his finger. "I want to talk to her first to make sure we're right."

"I'm past talking. We can't let this fester."

"Don't you care about her? You can get rid of her just like that?"

"This is business." Ramon stomped to the door. "Like Luca used to say, business always comes first."

CHAPTER TWENTY-FOUR

Milan's bedroom was like a suite at the Hilton, split into many of its own compartments.

First, there was the actual room where he slept. Then around the corner he had his own man cave with pool tables and more games than an arcade. Around another corner sat a living room area with a Jacuzzi, an office and a private kitchen with every amenity known to man.

Diana lay flat on the suede sectional in the living room space, staring out the window at the Victorian-style, high-security gate which shielded Milan from outsiders. "This is ridiculous."

"What?" Milan dangled his feet in the bubbling Jacuzzi as he jotted in his notebook.

"Your wealth. No one needs all this money."

"You just don't like money."

"It's not that I don't like money, but this is excessive, Milan. You could live to be two hundred and wouldn't spend all this."

He grinned, flipping a page. "You'd be surprised."

"I just don't get why one person needs all this shit."

"Newsflash, Anna." He smiled at her. "When men buy shit, it's not because we want it."

"I see. This is to impress women."

"It's to impress everyone. In my line of work, impressing is important. It signals power." He lowered his head and continued writing. "Your father damaged you."

"Excuse me?"

"He's never been there for you and that's why you don't think you deserve the best but you do, Anna. I want to give it to you."

She pinched the arm of the sofa. "I'm aware."

"Are you going to let me?" He set the notebook aside and unbuttoned his shirt. "The offer still stands."

"To be with you?"

"Do you believe me when I say I love you?"

"I think you're *in* love with me." She wiggled her toes. "But love comes with knowing someone more than a month."

"Because you say so?" He raised his head, leering. "I don't live by your rules."

"You don't live by any rules."

He took off the shirt, the golden hue of his skin reminding her how long it had been since she felt the hardness of a man inside her. "Come here."

She walked to him with bated breath, and he took her hand.

"When I look at you I see all the beauty in the world." He lowered her beside him and kissed her. "You remind me of what true happiness is."

"Do you trust me now?"

He shook his feet in the water. "Yes."

"I need to trust you too, Milan."

He kissed her hand, exhaling. "I'd never hurt you."

"I'm different from Celestina." She flattened her fingertips against his firm pecs. "I need to know everything about you and what you do."

His forehead wrinkled.

"Shielding me only puts me in more danger." She held his face, turning it toward hers. "If you trust me you'll let me in completely." She gave him an electrifying kiss that even surprised her at how hot it was. "I need that from you before I make any promises." She kicked off her flats and stuck her feet in the bubbles. "That's how it has to be."

"No one gives me ultimatums yet I put up with it from you." He chuckled. "I *must* be in love."

"I want to be able to ask you anything." She put her hand in the water and smoothed the wetness against his cheek.

He moaned, closing his eyes. "There's something on your mind."

She held her breath, hoping to God she didn't blow this but she couldn't wait any longer. "Who is George Wayans?"

He opened his eyes with an unresponsive gaze.

She kissed him again, hoping to steer his mind from suspicion. "I heard Ramon and Ivan mention him a few times."

He remained impassive.

She shrunk back, her hands trembling. "Forget it."

"He's no one."

"I've been coming around here a while now and every time I do, I hear his name. Seems like he's very important to you. Are you looking for him?"

"He's an associate. Or he *was*."

"He was a member of the organization?"

He scratched his nose. "Just someone to handle things for me when I needed an outsider."

"Did you fall out?"

"He did something horrible, and he needs to pay." Milan pulled her into his embrace. "Nothing more and nothing less."

"Are you going to kill him?"

He pinched her chin, slipping his tongue into her mouth.

"It's hard to think of you as someone who can take someone's life."

He gave her mouth a sharp lick after another kiss. "I don't want to."

"You're the leader." She gripped his shoulders. "You can let it go if you want."

"Wayans took something from me I can never get back and he'll pay if I have to hunt him for the rest of my life. Now can we please stop talking about George Wayans?"

"I always wanted to ask you, if you weren't in the mafia, what would you be doing?"

"Hmm." He massaged her knee. "No one's ever asked me that."

"How about being an author? Publish your work for the masses?"

His eyes twinkled. "Nah."

"You've thought about it." She nudged him with her elbow. "I see it in your eyes."

"No one would buy anything from me." He raised an eyebrow. "I'm a killer, remember?"

"You can use a pen name. How come you never let me see your writing?"

"You never asked."

She reached across his lap and got the notebook. "May I?"

He nodded appearing scared and flattered at the same time.

His latest poem began as apathetic as if he'd let go of his deepest emotions and then turned into a tidal wave of despair, guilt and self-pity. Every word dripping with longing as if he were entitled to love but accepted a life of loneliness.

By the time Diana got to the last unfinished word she'd began crying.

"I didn't mean to make you cry." He took the book. "Guess that's why I don't share them. Kinda pathetic, huh?"

"It's beautiful yet so sad." A tear trickled down Diana's cheek. "I can't give you what you're looking for."

"You already have." He lifted her blouse and caressed the cup of her bra. "Be with me."

"No."

"Why the fuck can't you?" He kissed her, forcing her forbidden fantasies into reality. "I want you in my bed and my life."

"What?" She panted, her vagina throbbing.

"I want you to stay in Miami."

"I have a life in LA."

"You can have a better one here." He kissed her arm, raising every hair on it. "Stay with me, Anna. Forever."

She drew her arm back. "No."

"Is there another man?" He yanked his feet out the water. "Eric?"

"No." She stood, getting her shoes. "I'm going back to the hotel."

He took her wrist. "Don't lie. I see the way he looks at you."

"You're wrong."

"You want me. What the hell is the problem?"

"Fuck, yes, I want you." She grabbed her head. "And it's killing me."

"It doesn't have to kill you." He smashed his lips over hers. "You can have me anytime you want."

"I can't." She pushed him away, sniffling. "This isn't me. None of this is me."

He scrunched his face. "You're not making sense."

"None of it makes sense. I'm going crazy because of you! You got me tearing my hair out."

"Good because that's how you make me feel."

"I wish everything was like it was before I met you. I don't even know who I am anymore."

"You're the woman I love." He seized her. "The woman I want to spend the rest of my life with. The woman I wanna marry."

"You're crazy." She punched his chest. "Let me go."

"You belong with me. Listen to your heart."

"Get off." She shoved him. "I don't want this. Don't you hear me? I don't!"

"Why?"

"This wasn't supposed to happen." She sobbed. "I never expected to like the person you are inside. To find you charming or sensitive."

"But you have. You can rationalize it all you want but it happened and it won't go away even if you go back to Los Angeles. You cannot control your heart, Anna. What do you want? What can I do to have you for good?"

"Nothing." She wiped her eyes with her palms. "Please get the driver to take me back."

"Running away won't change how you feel." He called out, "Reginald?"

The guard walked from around the corner. "Yes, sir?"

"Tell Kenny to get the car ready to take Ms. Hampton to her hotel."

Reginald nodded and left.

"Let me love you," Milan told Diana. "Please, don't shut me out."

Not able to bear looking at him, Diana walked to the doorway. "I'll wait for Kenny in the foyer."

CHAPTER TWENTY-FIVE

The second Eric walked toward Pam's boat his cop senses went in overdrive. Something was wrong, and her parted front door confirmed that. "Hello?" He knocked, peeking through the little window in the door. "Pam, it's me, Eric. Are you here?"

He took his gun from his pocket and eased inside, casing out the kitchen and den.

No sign of struggle. Everything seemed in place.

"Pam?" He walked through the hall and found a hysterical Douglas in the doorway of Pam's bedroom.

Douglas stared at him with red, teary eyes and went back to pacing and moaning as if Eric weren't there.

With their locked eyes came a sacred connection. Even kindred and Eric knew.

Douglas was a *cop*.

Douglas continued pacing, his black suede loafers leaving perfect impressions in the carpet.

Pam laid on her bed in a purple nightgown with her eyes pointed to the ceiling and her arms spread over the floral sheet.

"Ah!" Douglas kicked the wall. "No, no, no." He shoved items off the dresser. "Fuck!"

Eric examined the deep, red marks covering Pam's dainty neck indicating she'd been strangled.

"Milan did it," Douglas roared. "Course he isn't man enough to do it himself. Sent one of his boys to do it." He kicked in midair. "God damn him. I'm gonna kill that son of a bitch."

"Did you call the police?"

"Just get away from her." Douglas pushed Eric from the bed. "Stay away!"

"Okay." Eric stood against the wall, holding his palms out to him. "Calm down."

Douglas settled down, his gaze signaling that spiritual connection again. "She didn't deserve this, man. I loved her. Everything I did, was to make things better for her, for us."

Eric nodded.

"She was the shining light in this shit. The only thing that kept me sane." Tears hung from Douglas' eyelids. "She's dead because of me."

"Why?"

"I'm the leak." Douglas patted his chest. "I'm FBI."

Eric exhaled, touching his chin. "I'm betting Pam told you who I am."

Douglas gave a slight nod, sniffling. "I figured anyway. You got that cop look."

Eric sighed, still not knowing what that meant. "You know Anna is Diana Wayans?"

Douglas brushed tears away. "Yes."

"I'm so sorry about Pam. She was a sweet person."

"Milan thought Pam was the leak. I'll never, *ever* forgive myself." Douglas walked to the bed. "She laid her life on the line for me, and I didn't protect her like I promised. She was innocent in all this." He

leaned over her body. "It should've been me. I should be the one dead."
He lay beside her, wailing.

"I might be a detective and you FBI but we're cut from the same
cloth. Look at me."

Douglas did, face torn with sadness.

"Keep your head," Eric said. "It's duty before anything else now.
Getting Milan is even more important."

"I bet Ramon killed her." Douglas stood from the bed,
straightening his black T-shirt. "I'm bringing all their asses down." He
stomped out the room.

"Hey." Eric sprinted up behind him. "Where are you going?"

Douglas pushed Pam's loveseat out the way when they got to the
living room. "To kill Ramon."

"No, no, no, wait." Eric grabbed his arm. "You can't. It won't solve
anything."

"The fuck it won't." He pushed Eric and marched to the door. "It'll
make me feel a lot better."

Eric leaped in front of him. "I understand how you feel."

"Fuck you do. I just lost the woman I love. Have you experienced
that? Until you have don't come to me with your bullshit."

"I love Diana so much I'd rather die than something happen to her.
I understand how you feel."

"Diana's still here and Pam's not."

"Okay, kill Ramon and then what? Think of all the time and effort
you put into this investigation. Pam would want you to fight until you
stop the organization for good."

"How can I go back and be around Milan acting like everything is
fine knowing he had Pam murdered?"

"By remembering how much you love Pam and how much she'd
want you to finish the job."

CHAPTER TWENTY-SIX

Ramon entered his beach house mansion, ignored the bodyguard at the front door and ran up the timber steps, holding onto the glass balustrade.

Gala, his pudgy housekeeper walked through the colossal white hallway sprinkled with black doors. "Ah, Mr. Sotolongo. You have a visitor—"

"Can you get the fuck out?"

She batted her brown, basketball-sized eyes. "Excuse me?"

He leaned down to her face. "Can...you...get...the...fuck...out?"

"Yes, sir." She squeezed the sheets in her hand. "I was going to change your sheets."

"I'll do it." He yanked them from her. "Bye."

"I'll be back tomorrow morning." She ambled toward the stairwell. "Right?"

He nodded, faking a smile.

She ran downstairs.

"Nosey-ass bitch." Ramon charged into his bedroom, threw the sheets on the bed and took off his Kenneth Cole shirt. He sniffed it, smelling Pam's perfume. He'd miss it and her but he couldn't let anything come between him being leader of the organization.

Not even love.

He climbed to the other side of his bed and opened the black nightstand, his fingers gliding over the high-gloss finish. "Come to papa." He grabbed the half-empty bottle of scotch and drank. "Come on, Ramon." He sat on the edge of the bed. "Shake it off. It was business." His eyes landed on the picture of Pam by his lamp.

Her mesmerizing eyes chastised him, her soul haunting him already.

He got the picture. "It's your fault. I loved you. You could've had everything along with me but you were stubborn." He tossed her picture in the trash, got his phone out and called Milan.

"Yeah?" Milan asked.

"It's done."

"What are you talking about?"

"Pam." Ramon lay back on the pillows with one leg hanging off the bed. "I took care of her tonight."

"Wait, a damn minute."

"I confronted her with the evidence I found and she couldn't deny it. She just stood there shaking as if she knew the end was coming."

"You killed Pam?" Milan yelled.

"It had to be done."

"Have you lost your mind? I give the orders, Ramon. You don't move unless I say so. Who the fuck do you think you are?"

"The man who's gonna run this organization when you're gone. You forget that?"

"I'm not gone yet. You killed Pam? How could you be so reckless? We didn't prepare. The FBI is already sniffing around and now we give them another body?"

"I took care of business when no one else did. You would've never gotten rid of Pam. You've grown soft since meeting Anna."

"What did you say?"

"You've been slacking with business."

"I haven't signed the papers making you leader yet, Ramon. Maybe I shouldn't."

"I didn't mean any disrespect, but this is what Luca would've done. She'd have given us up. Did you want that?" Ramon sucked the bottle. "I saved us. Where's my thanks?"

Milan sighed. "Were you careful?"

"I'm always careful." Ramon ended the call.

George walked through the doorway.

"Ah!" Ramon jerked, spilling scotch on his pants. "Fuck, George. Could've shot your dumb ass."

George hopped on the bed, crossing his legs at the ankles. "Missed me?"

"Gray told me the shit you been saying." Ramon wiped scotch off his lap. "I didn't sell you out, man."

George shook his feet. "I call bullshit."

"I'm loyal to you and Gray." Ramon held the scotch out to him. "Looks like you could use it."

"No."

"Don't be like that." Ramon guzzled a shot, glancing at George's patent leather combat boots. "Got some new kicks there ay, Georgie Boy?"

"Save the sweet talk for Gray. You can't run game on me. I was playing it way before you were born."

"Fuck, George." Ramon swatted George's thigh. "We're about to get everything we've ever wanted. It's not the time to be doing this second-guessing shit. Our plan will only be as strong as our bond. I don't know what the fuck else I can do to make you believe me."

"Heard you on the phone just now." George laid his head on the headboard. "Talking to Milan?"

"I got the leak tonight. I ain't too happy about it but nothing stands before business, right?"

"Who was it?"

"Pam."

George lifted his head. "You been doing crack?"

"I got a hold of some notes she had that proved it. She'd been monitoring us and writing everything we'd done. Only the feds would have the resources she did."

"You killed her?"

Ramon sucked his teeth. "After I fucked her."

"Goddamn it, man." George stood. "Pam was a sweet person."

"She was the *leak*."

"Pam wasn't FBI!"

"No, but she was working with them. Couldn't have her nosing around and ruin everything. I did what I had to do. When I become leader it benefits you too, remember?"

George paced, sniffling.

"Are you crying?"

"I liked Pam. She was one of the few people around here with a heart. How can you look at yourself?"

"I'm not looking at myself. I'm looking at you." Ramon batted his eyes. "Pam's dead. Move on."

"Don't you care about anyone but yourself?"

"The organization is all that matters." Ramon got off the bed. "No one's ruining this for me. I'm about to get more power and money than I've ever dreamed."

"What about love?"

Ramon smirked, shrugging. "I can *buy* it."

George huffed, shaking his head.

"The prize will be when I off Milan." Ramon squeezed the bottle. "He'll pay for ruining my life."

"*Ruined*?" George spread out his arms. "You live in this fuckin' palace by the beach, get all the women you want, have everyone at your beck and call and you got designer clothes from head to toe, if that's ruined then sign me up."

"I don't know how much longer I can stand being around him. It's hard as hell looking at his face and pretending I care about him when I want to skin him alive."

"Milan didn't kill your father."

"No, but Luca did." Ramon's eyes narrowed. "And I vowed I'd take everything away from Luca Vitale. I'll take his son, money, and power, and it'll be beautiful, man. What the fuck you doing here, anyway? We can't risk Milan knowing you're still in town."

"Just seeing what's going on. You and Gray are my only link to the inside now."

"Came to check on Anna?" Ramon winked.

"What?"

"Oh, wait. Gray didn't tell you about Anna Hampton?"

"Just that Milan's giving up everything in the world for her. Is that supposed to mean something to me?"

"I can't believe it." Ramon leaned over, laughing. "Gray's full of shit. He didn't tell you?"

"What the hell are you talking about?"

"Let me fill you in, Georgie Boy." Ramon slapped his arm around George's shoulders. "Your daughter has been down here, uh, shall I say, seducing Milan?"

George's eyes got so wide the whites showed.

"Uh-huh." Ramon giggled. "Yeah see, Anna is Diana."

"Please." George's cheeks lightened. "Please, tell me you're kidding."

"Nope. She's got Milan's dick wrapped around *all* her fingers, and he's loving every minute."

CHAPTER TWENTY-SEVEN

George grabbed Ramon. "You're lying."

"You better back the fuck up." Ramon shoved him. "Why would I care enough about your daughter to lie?"

"Oh, no, no, no, no." George paced, touching his forehead. "Jesus, this can't be true. Diana is not in Miami."

"She's pretending to be some art buyer from LA, and Milan's crazy about her. Gray is too." Ramon slurped scotch. "I didn't know your daughter was such a piece of ass."

"Watch it."

"She's got Milan giving up the organization for her and Gray willing to cut off a body part if she looked his way. I wouldn't mind hitting that either. Thought Gray told you she was here."

"Gray didn't tell me shit. Got me walking around here and I don't know my baby girl's in the belly of the beast. Milan better not lay a finger on her."

"Chill. The last thing on Milan's mind is hurting her. It's unbelievable how much she controls him."

"Playing with Milan's heart?" George scowled. "What the hell is Diana thinking?"

"She's just like her daddy." Ramon leaned back on the dresser. "Ain't got no sense."

"Where is she staying?"

"You can't go to a hotel and risk Milan finding out you're still in town."

"I don't care."

"Well, I do." Ramon clutched the dresser. "Not letting you ruin this so you can have a Dr. Phil moment with a kid that couldn't care less about you."

"Shut up. Don't you have a heart at all? I gotta talk her out of this."

"If she's as stubborn as you are, good luck."

"Please." George grabbed him. "Help me."

"What the fuck am I supposed to do?"

"She's my daughter, Ramon. I'd die if something happened to her."

"Okay." He scratched his cheek. "I'll get someone to bring her here so you guys can talk."

"Thanks, man." George hugged him.

"Enough with all that." Ramon pushed him, grinning afterwards. "I hope she stays."

"You can't be serious."

"The longer she keeps Milan busy, the better for us."

"I KNEW THERE WAS SOMETHING about you." Diana stood at the metallic blue island in Douglas' frosted-gray kitchen the next morning. "Didn't know you were FBI though."

"He said I got that 'cop look,'" Eric stated from the connecting den with his feet propped on the marble table. "What the heck does that mean?"

Douglas poured coffee, his shoulders shaking as he grinned at Eric's question. "Here you go." With his dreads piled into a lazy man bun, he set two cups of cinnamon coffee in front of Diana.

She took her cup and blew into it. "Aren't you having any?"

"Nah." He swung two loose dreads out his eyes.

Eric scampered to the kitchen and got his cup. "Thanks."

Diana stirred the coffee with the little spoon. "Not much of a coffee drinker but I could use something to relax me that's for sure."

She and Eric sipped from their mugs while looking at each other.

Douglas walked across the slick, walnut wood floor and into the den. He cleared magazines and a newspaper off his white, leather La-Z-Boy.

"Magazines, newspapers," Diana said. "Don't like the Internet?"

"I'm old fashioned." Douglas set them on the black stand by his entertainment system. "Not into all those gadgets and things."

"Not into gadgets?" Eric snickered, exiting the kitchen. "Yet FBI works with the most sophisticated gadgets around."

"That's my work." Douglas tapped his long, bare foot. "I'm a simple person otherwise."

"You fit into Milan's lifestyle so well," Diana said. "It's hard to tell you weren't born into money."

"Don't let those fancy suites and Prada shirts fool you. I'm just playing the game to fit in. Besides, Milan bought me all that stuff."

"What aren't you living in a mansion like the others?" Eric sat in the recliner. "No offense, but this place looks like it cost less than mine."

Douglas crossed his arms. "Milan offered me a mansion on the beach but I refused."

Diana sat up straight on the kitchen stool. "Was he suspicious about that?"

"At first but the fact that I'm not money hungry like the others is what he likes about me the most."

"I'm so sorry about Pam," she said. "I can't imagine how you feel."

Douglas's eyes watered but he shook his head and any evidence of tears disappeared.

"How long have you worked for the Feds?" Diana asked.

"Four years. Joined the bureau at thirty-four."

"I toyed with the idea of joining the FBI," Eric said. "But being a detective takes so much out of me already that I wasn't willing to give up my whole life for the government."

"It's hard work, but it has its perks," Douglas said.

"Yeah, but being a fed is even more demanding than being a detective. Can't have any relationships or make time for anything."

Diana sipped coffee and swallowed. "You mean like when we were together?"

Eric jerked his head toward her. "Come again?"

"You barely had time for me when we dated."

Douglas raised his eyebrows.

Diana swayed on the stool. "Had to play Twister to get time with you."

"That's not true." Eric wiggled in the chair. "I made time."

"You didn't make enough time."

"You never told me I didn't."

"Yes, I did." She smiled. "You didn't listen."

"I *made* time. You were more important than any job."

Douglas winced, checking his watch.

Diana rolled her eyes and looked at Douglas. "How long have you been investigating Milan?"

"Two years."

"You must be damn good for the feds to put you on a big fish like Vitale," Eric said.

"How do you separate yourself?" Diana asked. "The real you from the facade? I'm struggling with that."

"Remember why you're doing what you're doing," Douglas said. "Don't let Milan sidetrack you. He's a master manipulator but you always have to remember what's at stake."

She nodded.

"He really cares about you," Douglas said. "Which makes what you're doing even more dangerous. One thing Milan doesn't play with is his heart and he doesn't like when it gets broken."

"Tell her he'd kill her if he found out who she was." Eric pointed to Diana. "She doesn't believe me."

"He's right," Douglas said. "Leave it alone. Investigating the biggest kingpin in the south is way above a paygrade of a graphic designer."

"And if the life of someone *you* loved was on the line, can either of you say you wouldn't do the same?"

The men dropped their shoulders.

"I rest my case. Did you know my father's in Miami still?"

"No." Douglas stuck out his neck. "Who told you this?"

"Gray."

"What the hell does Gray have to do with your father?"

"I was hoping you could tell me that." Diana carried her cup into the den.

Eric took a loud sip of coffee. "Gray and Ramon are hiding George from Milan."

"What?" Douglas grimaced.

"My father's been to Gray's recently, and at Milan's party, Eric overheard he and Ramon talking about seeing George."

Douglas blew a quick breath. "I don't know what that's about."

"Can't you use any of your resources to find George?" Eric asked.

Douglas chuckled. "The feds don't have little green men with radar that can tell us where someone is. Besides, knowing George he's probably left Miami by now."

"He's still around." Diana rocked. "I can feel it."

CHAPTER TWENTY-EIGHT

"George, Gray and Ramon seem mighty close." Eric peered at Douglas. "Are they friends?"

"Gray and Ramon have always been kinda close but I don't know what that has to do with George or why they'd be hiding him. I'll see what I can find out about George. Maybe I'll hear something through the grapevine."

Diana held her breath. "Why does Milan want to kill him?"

"Sorry." Douglas gestured to the pinewood door with fancy carvings. "Gotta cut this short."

"Douglas." Diana put her mug on his TV. "Please tell me why Milan wants my father dead."

"If you want my expert advice, go back to Atlanta, Diana." He opened the door and stepped aside. "I have to be in this mess, you don't. Save yourselves why you still can."

"I don't believe this." Diana followed Eric to the door and faced Douglas. "You're not gonna tell me?"

"Come on, Di." Eric tapped her arm. "Let's go."

Diana shook her head as she and Eric stepped on the porch.

"I took an oath to do what's right and to protect," Douglas said. "I can't put a civilian in the line of fire."

"So you won't help me?"

"You don't get it. It's not just your life at stake here. It's his." Douglas pointed to Eric. "It's your mother's, your friends and family. If Milan finds out you're lying to him, he'll take revenge out on everyone you care about."

She swallowed.

"This isn't just about George anymore." Douglas switched his gaze to Eric. "It's about the lives of everyone you love. Are you willing to sacrifice *them*? Is George that important to you?"

Diana thought about the question.

"Think about it." Douglas closed the door.

"He's right," Diana whispered. "I'm sacrificing everything for George. A man who doesn't seem to care anything about me."

Eric scratched under his bangs, his elbow hitting Douglas's hammock. "What you're doing shows what a great person you are. If it were my father I'd be doing the same thing." He followed her down the wooden steps. "Did you mean what you told Douglas?" Eric stopped her at their rented Honda. "That I didn't make time for you when we were together?"

She opened the passenger door. "It's old news."

"No." He held the door closed. "Just tell me."

"Everything was fine."

"You wouldn't marry me so *something* wasn't fine."

"Eric." She touched him and he moved out the way. "You were fine. We broke up because of me, remember?" She got in the car, whispering to herself, "Because I'm a fool."

THE NEXT EVENING, ERIC and Diana arrived at Ramon's beach house mansion surrounded by multiple terraces and hovering palm trees.

Eric stopped the car at the white security gate and whistled. "Shit, I should see if Milan would hook me up with a job."

Diana nudged him, snickering.

"Seriously. If I can make bank like this."

"Remember how they make that bank." Diana fixed her seatbelt. "I'd rather be broke the rest of my life."

"I'm sure you will be, Di."

She laughed, hitting his arm. "Shut up."

The gate opened and Eric drove through the pebbled driveway, which split in two directions. "I don't like this."

"Well, you should've stayed at the hotel like I told you to. I didn't need a babysitter."

"You get a weird invite to come to Ramon's and I'm gonna let you come alone." He parked and honked the horn. "Right, Diana. You said he was looking at you like you were a pork chop at Milan's party."

She got goosebumps, giggling. "Oh, so you came because you're jealous?"

"No." He smacked his lips. "I came to protect you."

She nodded. "Because you're jealous."

A pudgy, dark-olive skinned woman with high cheekbones scampered out of the house. "Miss Hampton?"

"Yes." Diana waved.

"I'm Gala." Her Italian accent became present on certain words. "Mr. Sotolongo told me to show you inside."

"Oh." Diana exchanged a bewildered glance with Eric. "Isn't Ramon here?"

"No, he has business to take care of."

"Then why did he want me to come?"

"Please, this way." Gala flashed a wide-toothed smile and dashed inside the house.

"I don't know about this, Di." Eric and Diana exited the car, taking measured steps past the circular bushes. "What if this is a set up?"

"Why would Ramon set me up?"

They hopped on the huge veranda.

"Maybe he knows who you are."

"Shit." Her breath skipped. "You think Gray told?"

"I don't know what the hell's going on but be prepared for anything."

They went inside the indigo, art décor door.

A burly black dude with a cantaloupe head and tight corn rolls guarded the door.

Diana checked out Ramon's living room. "Holy moly."

It was a stark-white open space with floor-to-ceiling windows from east to west.

The only color belonged to the blue door and the black and white diamond tile flooring.

Everything shined and glimmered from the icy crystal fixtures to the silver edges on the chandelier.

There wasn't any furniture until you crossed the huge medallion circle in the center of the floor and walked underneath the stairwell.

Suede, indigo furniture and sharp, art deco sculptures sprinkled around the living room.

Ramon's intrusive cologne didn't cover up the aquatic odor that came from living less than a mile from the beach.

"Can't believe he has all these windows," Eric said as they walked back to the foyer. "Not very secure if you ask me."

"They're one-way, bulletproof windows," the guard announced with a gruff voice as if he'd awaken from the dead. "We can see out but no one can see in."

"Ah." Eric nodded. "What's your name again?"

The guard switched his eyes ahead.

"Where is Ramon?" Diana asked him.

He ignored her too.

"I don't like this, Di. Let's get out of here."

"No," she called to Eric before he reached the door. "This could be about my father."

"Ramon's not even here. I'm getting that feeling that something is wrong so let's get the hell out of here."

"No."

"Diana, let's go."

"No, Eric."

"Hey, baby girl," an all-too familiar voice announced.

Diana froze, holding her breath.

CHAPTER TWENTY-NINE

Diana refused to turn around.

George walked up behind her and the hairs rose on her arms the same way they did when she first met Milan.

Eric gaped with his mouth wide open.

George touched Diana's shoulder and she trembled. "Aren't you gonna say hello to your daddy after all this time?"

Diana stayed put, terrified at looking George in the eyes. Afraid she'd weaken to his charms because all women did in George's presence. He was a gorgeous man with a sharp mind and velvet tongue that could have you believing any damn story he spun and that's what made him so dangerous.

"Okay." He put his lengthy arms around her, nudging her into his embrace.

"Get off me." She pushed him away, finally getting the courage to look into the same hazel eyes she saw in the mirror every day. "Where the hell you been?"

"Damn." He rubbed his hands, having the nerve to have a diamond ring on big as the Grand Canyon. "It's like looking in a mirror."

"He ain't lying," Eric said. "You look just like your daddy, Di."

George held that crooked grin. "Are you, Eric? She told me about you the last time I saw her."

"You mean in two thousand and eleven?" Diana asked. "None of your business who he is. And I didn't tell you about him, I mentioned him. Two different things."

"Yeah, I'm Eric."

George held his hand out to Eric. "George Wayans."

"I ain't shaking your hand." Eric frowned. "I'd like to kick your ass but not shake your damn hand."

George chuckled, tapping his nose. "You and who else because you ain't doing shit."

"I definitely should kick your ass. That's the least I can do after the shit you've put Diana through." Eric's nostrils flared. "You got the nerve to walk in here like it's no big deal? She's put her life in danger because of you."

George did a motion that reminded Diana he was left-handed. "Nobody asked her to."

"What?" She jerked. "You son-of-a-bitch."

"I didn't ask you to come here, Di."

"You bastard. I'm risking my life for you and that's all you can say?"

"What do you expect? Me to throw your ass a party? Di, you got no business being here."

"If it weren't for you she wouldn't be here."

George scowled at Eric. "This is none of your business."

"It is my fuckin' business."

"Eric." Diana jumped between them. "Stop."

"No, you're some piece of work, man." He pointed to George over Diana's shoulder. "You have a daughter who you didn't give a shit about who risked her life to help you and you aren't grateful?"

"Grateful for her putting herself in danger?" George yelled. "Di, you know this was a stupid thing to do."

"I do but not for the danger, because you don't give a damn about me."

"Oh, please. Don't nobody wanna hear that." He dismissively waved at her and strutted to the window with his boots half-laced. "I don't care about you, huh? That's why I called you to warn you?"

Eric shook his head. "You're pathetic."

"Man, who the fuck are you to judge me?"

"I'm the man she can count on, that's who." Eric bumped into Diana as he charged George. "I was the one who wiped her tears whenever she got upset because you missed another birthday or didn't care enough about anyone but yourself to call her."

"This is between us," George snarled. "Ain't got nothing to do with you. You better watch how you talk to me, son."

"I'm supposed to be scared of a coward?"

"I got your coward." George marched from the window. "Say that shit in my face."

"Stop!" Diana waved her hand to George while pushing Eric back. "Eric, calm down."

"No. This man is the reason we broke up."

"What?" George laughed. "I've been blamed for a lot of shit but this is ridiculous."

"She can't trust men because of you. If you had been a better father than she would've let me love her."

"If she didn't want your ass, it had nothing to do with me. I can see why she wouldn't want you."

"Stop it," Diana yelled. "Why am I here, George? Why?"

He panted, glaring at Eric while fixing his Armani shirt. "Hoping I could talk some sense into you."

"Ha!" Eric laughed. "You can't talk sense into someone if you don't have it yourself."

"You better get your boy, Di."

"Stop." She waved her arms. "Eric, please. I need to find out what's going on. Wait for me in the car."

"Hell no." He held his waist, planting his feet in the floor. "I'm not going any damn where. Not leaving you alone with this jerk."

"I'm her father, asshole."

"Oh, it's good you remembered."

George groaned, balling fists.

"Enough, Eric. I need to know what he wants."

"Then talk to him." He crossed his arms swaying. "I'm not leaving from this spot."

Diana sighed then turned toward George. "Talk. Why is Milan after you?"

George snapped his fingers at the guard. "Can you find something to do?"

The guard huffed, turned and disappeared around the corner.

"It's none of your business why Milan's after me, Di."

Eric scoffed.

"Maybe I don't have a right to tell you what to do." George straightened the dial of his silver and gold Swiss Rolex. "But you're getting your ass out of Miami before you end up in a body bag. Is that what you want?"

"I didn't just inherit your eyes, I got your stubbornness too, George. I'm not going any damn where until I know what's going on. I can't just go back home, anyway." She followed him as he walked back to the window. "I killed Ernesto. I'm sure Milan's got me on his hit list now too."

"*What?*"

"He attacked me."

"Jesus." George's eyebrows sagged with sincerity. "Are you all right?"

"I'm alive."

"Did he hurt you?"

"He almost killed her because of you," Eric said. "What a great dad you are."

"Please leave, Di."

"One of the most dangerous men in the world wants you dead." She moved closer to her father. "You won't tell me why? Then I ain't leaving."

"Telling you only puts you in this deeper. Don't you get it?"

"Milan's in love with me." She shrugged. "I can't get any deeper."

"Milan thinks I betrayed him, and he's not a man to let something like that go. I didn't do what he thinks I did, but he doesn't believe me so I had to run."

Eric squinted, inching toward them. "How in God's name did you get mixed up with the mob?"

"I see opportunities and I take them unlike some people. My god, Di." George touched his forehead. "He's given up the organization for you. How could you let it go this far?"

"I'd do anything for family unlike you. What's pathetic..." She shifted, fighting tears. "I'd do it all over again to save you."

"But you're not saving me, baby girl. You're putting yourself in danger and something happening to you would kill me faster than Milan could."

She cleared her throat, looking at the floor.

"I fucked up with you." George rubbed his hands. "I tried to run from the guilt but it's gotten worse. I just wasn't cut out to be a father, and I never wanted to be one."

She swallowed the pain that accompanied his words.

"I tried to make it work, but it was like putting a fish in the sand. It just wasn't me, Di." He sniffled. "I wanted so much to be a good husband and father."

"If it were up to you..." Her lips trembled. "I wouldn't have been born, huh?"

"No, that's not true. I love you. I was a fool when your momma and I got married." He tried to take her hand, but she moved. "We were barely in our twenties and couldn't make ends meet. It was the eighties. I got in the crack game and that was it."

"You were on crack?" Eric gaped.

"He sold it," Diana said. "That's why he went to prison for three years."

"You said he went for writing bad checks."

"Yeah, well I was too embarrassed to say my dad used to be a crack dealer."

"Shit, I wasn't no good at that either." George snickered. "My partner said it was easy money and I got caught the third time selling it. Sold to an undercover vice cop." He scratched his head. "My dumbass. But, I don't want to go into all that." He took Diana's hand, and it felt good to let him. "What I'm trying to say is, out of all the stuff I've done, my biggest regret is leaving you and your momma."

She clenched his hand.

"There's nothing I love more on this earth than you, Diana. I've caused you enough trouble that's why I can't let you do this. I'm trying to be better. That's why I'm still in Miami. I'm tired of running all the damn time from responsibilities. I gotta take care of this, Di. Me. It's my responsibility."

"I'm in this now." She let his hand go. "I can take care of myself."

"Why the hell do you have to be so stubborn? I'm trying to protect you."

"That's my job now," Eric said. "You gave up your right to protect her years ago."

Diana would usually be offended by a man suggesting she needed protection but coming from Eric she'd welcome the sentiment a million times over.

George stomped toward him. "I'd punch the fuck out of you if—"

"If what?" Eric stood tall.

George relaxed his shoulders. "If I didn't see how much you care about my daughter."

Eric's expression lightened.

George held his hand out to him. "Thank you."

Eric shook his hand, and Diana smiled.

"You're a good man, Eric. A man any father would want his daughter with."

"Want to do me a favor then?" A smile brightened Eric's lips. "Tell your daughter to give me another chance."

Diana cleared her throat to take away from her discomfort. "What happens now, George?"

"I got it covered." He winked. "Trust in your old man though I know I haven't given you reason to."

"Where are you staying?"

He touched her hair. "Around."

She sighed. "Just don't go disappearing again, okay? I mean, don't leave Miami unless you tell me."

"Oh, I'm not going anywhere until this is settled." He kissed her cheek. "You might see me again while you're here."

"Di, you ready to go?" Eric asked.

"Yeah." She watched George over her shoulder as she followed Eric to the door. "You got my number, George. Please, call me before doing anything stupid concerning Milan. Are you gonna be okay?"

"I'm always okay, Di. Hold on. I got something to give you." George dug in his pocket and took out a multicolored woven bracelet with tiny shells as pendants. "I got it from a tribe in Madagascar."

"You were in Africa?" Diana took it, marveling at the craftsmanship.

"Spent time in the rain forest down there." He raised his chin. "Became close with a tribe and they made me that as a symbol of friendship."

"It's beautiful. Feels like home. Like there's a connection."

Eric smiled when she looked at him.

"The chief told me to give it to someone who I wanted to make amends with and he says the Gods blessed the bracelet and it would make everything all right." George swallowed, teary-eyed. "No one else I'd rather have it than you."

"Thanks." She sniffed it, smelling the forest and jungle air.

"I hope one day we can get past all the shit I've done."

She gave no promises, just nodded. "Take care of yourself, George."

Diana and Eric walked out, and she exhaled so loudly she wouldn't have been shocked if they heard her back in Atlanta.

Eric examined the bracelet. "Can't believe an African tribe made this. Boy, you weren't lying when you said George gets around. Are you all right?" He gave her the bracelet back. "Must have a thousand emotions going right now."

"Yeah." She looked at the bracelet, feeling closure between her and George for the first time. "I'm okay."

CHAPTER THIRTY

A few nights later Diana almost couldn't breathe while dancing with Milan in his ballroom. She wasn't sure if it was because he held her so tightly or because of the anxiety she always got being close to him.

As the high-pitched, sultry crooning of Mary J. Blige swept them into romance, there was only one man she wanted to be this close to and he sat in a hotel room alone worrying like hell about her.

Milan's tongue wet her earlobe as he whispered, "You were made for me to hold you."

His grip on the curve of her back and how he pressed her into his chest as if he tried to mold her into him, told her tonight he might never let go. That no matter how much she resisted his advances, he might not listen. Or, maybe she might give into that curious ache that awakened whenever he held her.

She moved her head from his shoulder scared to death at not knowing what she'd do.

Milan's masculine shoulders flexed underneath the tight-fit, long-sleeved dress shirt. "You love this song, huh?"

"I love all her songs." Diana dropped one hand to his while keeping her other on his shoulder. "She's my favorite singer."

"I'm a Whitney man myself." He did a tiny chuckle. "Boy, do I miss her. What a talent the world lost."

"We're alone."

"Yep." A lovesick haze fell over his angelic eyes. "We've been alone before."

"Not like this." Diana peeked toward the doorway. "Without a bodyguard around the corner or your housekeepers walking around. What about Douglas? Is he here?"

"Why do you care about Douglas?"

She took in his oak fragrance. "I don't, but you've let down your guard tonight."

He kissed her nose, his fingertips burrowing into her back. "My guard's never down. I spent hours putting these roses on the walls. Do you like it?"

She smiled as he swayed her. "You shouldn't have gone to so much trouble."

"Tonight's been perfect." The gold buttons on his sleeve cuffs sparkled. "Every night with you is like a fairytale."

Diana released a tired sigh.

His brow twisted. "Something wrong?"

"No. Just tired."

"I hope not too tired because the date is far from being over." He twirled her in a swan-like move and held her close again.

"You're a good dancer. Very light on your feet."

"That's what private lessons will get you. My dad wanted me to be as cultural as possible." He rolled his eyes, smirking. "I'm trained in a variety of dance and music."

"You never told me that."

"My mission is to make every time we're together a surprise." He laid his lips on hers. "Why don't we take a swim under the moonlight?"

"I have nothing to swim in."

He snickered. "That's the point."

Her hands grew sweaty, and she hoped he wouldn't pick up on the tension.

He loosened his hold on her signaling he had picked up on it. "What's wrong, Anna?"

"What do you mean?"

"You've been distant tonight." His face glistened under the lights. "Did I do something wrong?"

"May I be honest?"

"I want nothing more." He turned toward the smart speaker. "Turn off Mary J. Blige."

The music stopped.

He unbuttoned the top button of his shirt. "What is it?"

"Tonight has been amazing." She touched the necklace he'd given her. "But is this how it will always be with us?"

"What do you mean?"

"We don't go anywhere because it's too dangerous for you. In all these dates, we've only gone to the museum and your yacht. I just...I don't know."

"I have to plan to go out and it takes a while to do that because I have to be sure it's safe."

"I feel like this is turning into *my* prison too. I love your home, but I want to go out."

"You can do anything here. I have a movie theater, a tennis court, an art room." He took her hands. "We need nothing but each other."

"I'm a social person. I can't just sit in the house all the time no matter how beautiful it is."

"Don't you think I want to go out like other people?" He pointed to the arched windows draped in red, velvet curtains. "Have a life outside the organization? Outside these walls? Anna, I'm doing the best I can. For most women it's more than enough."

"I couldn't breathe staying here all the time."

"We can go back to the yacht." His eyes drooped with sadness. "I'll have a party there and we can interact with people together—"

"That's not what I mean. You take vacations all over the world, don't you?"

"Yes, after planning them carefully. Do you enjoying yourself with me?"

"Yes."

"Then that's what's important." He touched her lips with his index finger. "I love you even more than I did Celestina."

"You can't mean that."

He kissed her as a shaky gasp escaped her lips. "Come on." He took her hand. "Let's go upstairs for the rest of your surprise."

IN MILAN'S BEDROOM, passionate saxophone music greeted them from a speaker underneath sultry lights.

Rose petals were everywhere.

On the bed, under their feet, on the slick, gold sheets.

Milan brushed up against her backside as he always did when he passed her and walked to the container of ice and champagne on the dresser. "You like it?"

Diana sat on the bed, roses dangling from the ceiling fan. "Are there any roses left in Miami?"

He laughed. "Maybe not."

"It's so romantic." She touched the necklace again. "Everything is so romantic."

He smiled at her over his shoulder while pouring the drinks.

"I hope I didn't hurt your feelings downstairs."

"No, and we promised to be honest with each other." He put the cork back in the bottle and carried two glasses to the bed. "Armand de Brignac Rose. Ever had it?"

"If you never gave it to me before I haven't."

He laughed as he sat next to her.

She sniffed the pink bubbly and took a sip. "Mm." At first the full-bodied freshness shocked her tongue then came a slow build of strawberries and silkiness. "Wow."

"Good?"

"Oh, it's better than good." She sipped more. "It's heaven."

"Should be. It's five hundred dollars a bottle."

Diana coughed, covering her mouth. "What?"

"Mm-hmm."

"Five hundred dollars for a bottle of fuckin' wine? Excuse my language but that's insane."

He winked, sipping. "That's luxury."

"What do they extract it from? Diamonds?"

"Only the best for you, Anna. This is a sample of what I can offer you. My home, my yacht, expensive champagne and yes, vacations if we plan them."

She smiled.

"You can have anything you want. I don't care what I have to do, I'll make it happen." He sucked remnants of champagne from his lips. "Before you, my world existed in my notebook. I lost Celestina, and then I lost my father thanks to George Wayans." He looked into the glass before drinking again.

Diana coughed a bit as she sipped. "George Wayans?"

"My father was everything to me." His face turned ghostly white which wasn't easy for a man of his complexion. "And George killed him."

CHAPTER THIRTY-ONE

Diana dropped her champagne. "Oh."

"Whoa." Milan rushed to the dresser and got the hand towel. "What happened?" He wiped sprinkles from her legs and shoes. "You okay?"

She blinked, focus fading in and out from shock. "George Wayans killed your father?"

"He poisoned him."

"I thought your dad died from dementia."

"We don't broadcast facts to the public. This is an internal issue, and I'll take care of it."

"Wait." Diana became lightheaded either from Milan's claim or the champagne. "How do you know George killed Luca?"

"We *know*." He sat beside her again and squeezed her hand. "I didn't bring you here to talk about this. I try my best to forget it."

"No, no. How do you know he killed your father?"

"I don't want to talk about this." He pushed her on the bed, plastering his lips over hers. "I don't want to talk at all."

"Mm." Diana pushed at him, mumbling against his soggy kisses. "Milan. Hold on."

"For what?" He panted with hunger in his eyes as he pushed up her dress and grabbed her thigh.

"Wait." She shoved his hand away but he kept going. "Milan, wait."

"Fuck." He punched the bed and climbed off her. "Fuck!"

"I'm sorry." She rose, noticing his erection. "I'm just not ready."

"Not ready?" He grabbed his crotch, maneuvering himself in his pants. "Not ready?"

"I'm sorry." She pulled her dress down, covering her thighs.

A growling grin escaped him. "She's still not ready."

"Please, Milan." She touched her hair, her ball had loosened from his actions. "I'm sorry."

He kept his head down, nodding. "I wanted you the night we went to the museum. I didn't expect it since we didn't know each other well. Fine. I waited." He balled fists, a fat vein popping from his neck. "I wanted you when you came back and back and back. You weren't ready."

She awkwardly grabbed roses off the sheet as frustration grew in his voice. "Milan."

"I wanted you on my yacht." He shot her a venomous glare. "You said no. I waited."

She closed her eyes, holding her breath.

"My party. After I announced leaving the organization to be with you." He lifted his hand like a king giving a grand speech. "Showed you around like a princess. Let everyone know how much I cared about you. I brought you up here, and you said no again. It made me mad, Anna. Madder than I'd been in a long time."

"I remember."

"I respected your wishes all those other times, but not tonight. I don't want 'no' on a night that's so damn special."

"Milan."

"Look at all these fuckin' roses I put up all over the goddamn place." He stomped around. "Hours and hours it took. Bringing out five hundred dollar champagne and I have to wait *again*?" He hurried to her and she got off the bed, backing away. "All this for you!" He raised his arms. "I've done everything I could to please you and nothing works."

"That's not true." She backed into the doors. "I appreciate everything you ever did."

"Yet, you tell me to wait again?" He stopped coming toward her, and she thanked God. "I've been waiting. Anna, I'm not waiting anymore."

"What are you gonna do?" Her bones quaked. "Force me?"

"No! I want you to want me too or there's no point to any of this. I need the truth here and right now." He slapped his hands together. "Will you ever be ready to make love to me? Is that what you want or not?"

She grabbed at her bodice, breathing heavily.

"Answer me." Something animalistic showed in his eyes. "Will you ever be ready? Do you love me, Anna?" He grabbed her. "Please, answer me. Do you *love* me?"

She closed her eyes, imaging what horror awaited her when she answered but she did, anyway. "No." She looked away from him. "I don't love you."

He unwrapped his fingers from her arms, rolling his tongue around in his mouth. "Gray was right. You just lead men on for kicks. You're sick."

"What do you want from me?"

"I've been honest with you and I want the same."

"No, you don't." She walked across the room. "You want what you want to hear."

"I want the truth!"

"Okay, here it is." She charged him. "No, I don't love you, Milan. I despise you."

He sunk back, squinting.

"I could never be with a man like you. You are a murderer. A monster."

He wobbled, batting his eyes.

"How dare you judge me for not sleeping with you with all the shit you've done? You sit here and whine about your life but you're the reason for it." She pointed at him. "You're lonely because of your actions. That's why we're here now and that's why you can't have me and it eats you up."

He closed his eyes, muscles moving in his jaws.

"All your life you've had everything you wanted. No one ever said no to you and what kills you is that I'm the one thing you will never, ever have."

He threw her on the bed. "I can have you if I want." He brought his mouth closer as she turned hers away.

"Thought you wouldn't force me."

"I don't *want* to."

"But you would? That's what your world's all about isn't it? Taking things. What has that gotten you, Milan?"

His eyelids sagged.

"You can take my body but you'll never have the one thing you want more than anything, my heart."

"Anna, please." He sobbed, clutching her face. "Don't do this to me. I love you."

She sniffled. "I am attracted to you and I fight every day not to be."

"Why fight it? Let go of it, Anna." He kissed her. "Please. Can we just be together? You can learn to love me."

"You can't learn love." She moved his arm away and sat up straight. "True love comes from deep in your soul."

"That's us." He kissed her hand. "I swear it's us, Anna. I'm all you need."

"I don't love you, Milan." She rose from the bed as his eyes shrunk with grief. "I never will."

CHAPTER THIRTY-TWO

George entered Ramon's living room after Gala informed him of a visitor.

Diana sat in the chair wearing a slim-fit, cocktail dress that stopped at the knees of her gorgeous legs.

"Man." He whistled. "You look like your mother with your hair up like that." He walked to her and plucked the rose petal from her bun. "Where'd that come from?"

She took it but didn't answer.

"You shouldn't be here, Di." He sat on the arm of her chair. "But, I'm glad to see you again. From the way you're dressed I'm guessing you had plans with Milan tonight? I wish you'd reconsider and call it off."

"It's over." She slipped the petal in and out her fingers. "I won't be going back to Milan's."

"Shit, does he know who you are?"

"No. He wanted me to sleep with him, and I refused. He got mad, and we had an argument."

"Did he hurt you?"

"No, but he was mad. He kept saying he loved me like I owed him something." She sighed. "He wouldn't let his driver take me back so I got a cab and came here so we could talk. He told me why he's looking for you."

George held his breath. "I didn't kill Luca."

"I know. You're a lot of things but a killer isn't one of them."

"Someone set me up. I went to see him and he was fine. The next morning, he was dead, and I'm running for my life."

"What kind of stuff did you do for Milan?"

He rubbed his thighs. "Stuff you wouldn't tell your daughter."

"Did you hurt someone for him? Did you lean on people for him?"

"No."

"What's between you, Gray and Ramon? Why are they hiding you from Milan? Did Ramon have something to do with Luca's death?"

"Why you say that?"

"Luca's death gets Ramon one step closer to running Vitale. That's all he ever talks about."

"Just leave it alone, Di. You're digging in stuff that's not your business."

"You don't trust Ramon, do you?"

"Sh." George pointed toward the ceiling. "He has cameras. If Ramon thinks you're any threat to what he's doing, he'll kill you."

"Like he killed Pam?"

"Exactly." He stood. "If he can kill a woman he had a relationship with then what do you think he could do to you?"

She snatched his hand. "Tell me what you got going with Ramon and Gray."

"We're partners." He cleared his throat. "Ramon splits everything with me and Gray once he owns the empire. I'm about to be a very, very rich man, Di."

"So you made a deal with the devil?"

"This is the real world, Di, not some fairytale." He bounced his head. "You believe that all you have to do is make the right choices or work hard and you'll get rewards well that's bullshit. How do you think Milan's family got so damn powerful?"

"And that's something you aspire to be like?"

"This is me, Di." He patted his chest. "I'm one of the bad guys. Deal with it."

"You don't have to be."

"It is what it is. Go back home and back to your life and let me take care of business. Isn't that what you always wanted me to do?"

"Fine." She huffed as she stood. "Momma couldn't ever talk sense into you so why would I be different?" She passed the bodyguard as she walked to the front door.

"Wait." George ran behind her, taking her hand.

She whimpered, lips shaking. "Will I see you again?"

"Of course." He pinched her cheek. "Next time I'm in Atlanta I'll buy you dinner."

"Sounds like you did when I was a kid. Telling me you'd come take me somewhere and never show. I can't take anymore empty promises, George. I'm too old and tired for that."

"It's not empty." He kissed her forehead, savoring her touch because he hadn't a clue how long it would be before he held her again. "Go back to Atlanta and take care of Eric. Give him another shot. He loves you."

"Promise me you'll be safe."

"I promise."

"My taxi's waiting."

The guard opened the door for her.

"Take care, George." She stared at him as if it might be the last time.

"Di?" he blurted out as she stepped onto the porch. "Thank you. For everything."

She nodded and walked to the cab.

George watched as the taxi vanished in the darkness. "I love you."

CHAPTER THIRTY-THREE

Ramon entered Milan's office, breathing in the earthy aroma of aged scotch sitting on the table.

"Goddamn it!" Milan threw a chair across the room. "Fuck!"

Ramon kept his distance. "What the hell's wrong with you?"

"What's wrong is that I lost myself." Milan yanked his half-empty glass off the table and guzzled. "I forgot who the fuck I am because of her."

Ramon inched toward him. "Anna?"

"Who else?" Milan stared at him, face dripping in desperation. "Everyone was right about her and I was a fool."

"Because you fell for her?"

"No, because instead of taking charge I let her go." Milan pointed his glass toward the doorway. "I let the best thing that's happened to me since Celestina walk out the door and why?" He rushed to Ramon, widening his eyes. "Because I forgot who I was but no more. No more, Ramon. I'm back." Milan straightened his spine. "I'm Milan Vitale and I run this organization!"

For now.

"*I* rule this kingdom." Milan pounded his chest. "Anna can't leave me."

"Wait, wait, wait. She's gone?" Ramon stood at the table surrounded by imported chairs made of Italian wood. "What, she dumped you?"

"No one dumps Milan Vitale!"

"What the hell happened?"

"I got angry." Milan's voice settled and his breathing leveled out. "I told her to get out but didn't mean it. I'd planned to make love to her tonight. Everything was perfect."

"This explains all the damn roses in the hallway."

"I put those up myself. Look at my fingers." Milan showed off the reddish tips. "All day I was stapling, nailing and taping roses and did it get me anywhere, no? She thinks I'll let her walk away." He grinned. "No way. She's not leaving me holding my heart in her hands."

"Let it go. She's just a woman."

"She's everything, and I'm nothing without her." Milan dropped into a chair. "She made me happy again. Made remember how to be a man and not just the leader of an empire."

Ramon's heart sunk as Pam's beautiful face pushed its way into his head. "You're in love. I get it."

Milan lifted his notebook off the table. "She's taken everything from me. I need her to even survive."

"Forget Anna. More important things we need to talk about."

"I'd have given her anything." Milan nibbled the rim of his glass. "Anything she could ever want. Most women would kill for this. I've been thinking about all the things I've lost because of this organization. How I sacrificed my happiness all these years."

"It was your duty to your family. Where I come from, family is everything."

"She can't leave me." Milan's eyes gleamed from authority. "She's gonna come back because I say she will."

"You knew the woman a month."

"What the hell am I trying to get you to understand for?" Milan scoffed. "You killed the woman you loved."

Ramon exhaled through his nostrils. "Luca taught you to be a soldier. That nothing mattered beyond the organization."

"He was wrong. Ramon, you got to want more from life than money and power."

"Fuck, no!" He slapped the table. "That's more than enough then again I didn't come from money, remember? I had to fight and hustle for everything I had."

"Is that a dig toward me?"

"You're pathetic." Ramon strutted on the maroon carpet. "Always have been and always will be."

"What?"

"You've had more happiness than you ever deserved. More than I ever had because I had to sit there for years and look at your face when all I wanted to do was break every bone in it!" He grabbed Milan out the chair and punched him.

"Fuck." Milan spit blood, wobbling. "What the fuck is wrong with you?"

"Shut up." Ramon took out his gun and aimed it at him. "You're listening to me now."

"Have you gone crazy?" Milan panted, wincing. "You must be out of your mind to pull your gun on me."

"Shut up!"

"Are you *insane*?"

"No." Ramon pressed the trigger. "But I almost became that way pretending to care about you and your family all these years. It made me sick."

A bead of sweat divided Milan's forehead.

"It's judgement day, pussy." Ramon bared his teeth. "I hate you, Luca and everything Vitale stands for."

"I don't know what the hell is going on here but if you pull that trigger you'll be dead too because my guards will—"

"You mean *my* guards." Ramon smiled. "They do what I say because I'll be leader soon. A lot sooner than you realized."

CHAPTER THIRTY-FOUR

R amon pressed his gun against Milan's forehead. "Say my name."
Milan scowled. "What?"

"Say my fuckin' name." He pushed Milan against the table. "Say...my name."

"If you're going to kill me, do it." Milan spit in his face. "I'm not begging you for my life."

"Don't you want to know why I'm doing this?"

"Because you're what Douglas says you are. A coward with no loyalty." Milan waved his hand. "He was right about you all along and I couldn't see it."

"Say my name and I'll tell you why I hate you."

Milan huffed and puffed, eyes shifting from left to right. "Ramon."

"No, my name's not Ramon." Ramon shook him, sweat dangling from the tip of his nose. "My mother didn't name me Ramon."

"Then who the fuck are you?"

"Glad you asked." He slammed Milan into a chair and turned him loose. "October fifteenth, nineteen-ninety-two six p.m. Where were you?"

"How the fuck should I know? I was ten!"

Ramon aimed the gun at Milan's face.

Milan breathed, clenching his lips together. "I was here after I'd finished with the tutor probably. Homeschool was over around four. What the fuck is going on?"

Ramon rocked from side to side. "Know where your daddy was that night?"

"I was a kid. All I cared about was when he came home not when he was gone."

"Did you ever wonder?"

"*No.*" Milan glared at him. "Why would I?"

"I didn't have to wonder where my dad was because I was right there in the house with him."

Milan groaned. "Good for you."

Ramon's hands shook as that inner agony that owned him for years resurfaced. "Luca was there too."

"My father didn't meet you until you were eighteen."

"I didn't say he *met* me that day. I said he was at our house. Two different things."

"Keep playing this game." Milan thrust his finger in Ramon's face. "You want me to beg for my life? Fuck you. I don't deserve this."

"You deserve this and more." Ramon laughed. "And your daddy deserved what he got just as much."

Milan lunged at him but stopped when Ramon raised the gun.

"Oh, come on, Milan. Don't make me have to shoot you now when the fun's just starting. Does the name Federico Bastiani ring a bell?"

"He worked for my father for years. What does this have to do with you?"

"He worked for him until that day in October nineteen ninety-two." Ramon searched Milan's face for a sign that the lightbulb had come on yet. "Remember?"

Milan shrugged, rolling his eyes.

"Federico was my father, and Luca killed him."

"What?" Milan stumbled back. "No, no, dad loved Federico like a brother. He'd never hurt him. Federico was your father?"

"Luca thought my father was embezzling from Vitale but my dad wasn't a thief. My guess is someone else in the organization blamed him to keep Luca's eyes off themselves. Luca killed my dad."

"You're lying."

"I was right in the next room. I still hear the gunshots every time I close my eyes to sleep." Ramon grabbed Milan. "You wanna know where I was that night? I was ten too, and hiding under a bed so your daddy wouldn't kill me."

"No." Milan closed his eyes, sniffling.

Ramon shook him. "Hiding, listening to the gunshots, and hearing my dad's lifeless body fall to the floor."

"Liar." Milan shoved him. "I won't listen to this bullshit."

"Yeah, you don't like hearing about the real Luca, do you?"

Milan turned away from him.

"You wanna keep blocking out all the horrible things he did, but Luca was the monster everyone says he is. Your father would've kill me, a helpless ten-year-old boy. I hid in the closet, behind the clothes for hours jumping at every sound until he left. I came out and saw my father on the living room floor, swimming in blood. Face mutilated from the shot."

Milan shook his head, pulling his hair.

"I kept shaking him." Ramon swallowed. "I kept screaming and begging for him to wake up but he didn't move. That one day I lost everything. I didn't have anyone but my father. That's all the family I had."

"No!" Milan shook his fists.

"And you just turned a blind eye to the shit Luca did because being rich made up for it."

"I don't give a shit about money."

"Sure you don't because you've always had it. If you knew what it was like to be poor you'd care."

Milan's forehead creased above his brows. "Who are you to judge my father with all the blood on *your* hands?"

"I lost everything when my dad was killed." A tear rolled over Ramon's cheek. "I went through a hundred foster homes until I was eighteen. All I could think about was revenge. My plan was to get Luca to trust me so I could take everything from him."

"You killed my father."

"Yes."

"Damn you."

Ramon sucked a tear from his lip. "As I pumped that poison into Luca's veins I made sure my father's death was the last thing on his mind."

"You won't get away with this."

"The fuck I won't." Ramon smiled. "I made sure I'd own everything that meant something to Luca. His trust, his love, his empire."

"You'll never get your hands on everything my father's built."

"You're just like him." Ramon tilted his head. "No remorse at all."

"Remorse?" Milan hollered. "I don't feel sorry for you at all. I'd apologize to the little boy who had to hide under that bed but you're not that little boy anymore. You're an evil man, and I don't owe you a damn thing."

"Now who's judging?" Ramon chuckled. "Should we line up the dead bodies that have *your* name on them? I'd bet your pile would be a lot bigger than mine."

"My father was loyal to you. He brought you here and gave you a home. Gave you love."

"Is that supposed to erase what he did?" Ramon's voice cracked. "If the shoe were on the other foot you'd be standing right here too. I'm doing what Luca taught me. What kind of leader would I be if I don't take care of business?"

Milan got closer to him and breathed in Ramon's face. "You'll be dead before you walk out of here."

"No, you'll be." Ramon patted Milan's cheek. "And I'll get everything."

Milan widened his stance, sticking out his chest. "Never."

"Oh, there's another twist to the story." Ramon wiggled his eyebrows. "I killed Celestina too."

Milan just stared at him, his face turning red as if years of anger, anger Ramon knew too well, pushed its way inside him. Before Ramon could guess Milan's next move, Milan latched his sturdy hands around Ramon's neck and slammed Ramon's head into the table.

The gun flew out Ramon's hand as he shuddered from the dizzying pain of his teeth stabbing into his tongue.

"You bastard." Milan slammed his stone-hard fist into Ramon's jaw. "Oh!"

With each punch, life drained from Ramon and he imagined his father standing before him, urging his son to continue the mission.

CHAPTER THIRTY-FIVE

"You're dead!" Milan pounded Ramon, feeling Ramon's face swelling underneath his fist.

"Go on." Ramon gurgled, spewing dark blood. "You can't kill me because I'm already dead. I died when Luca killed my father."

Milan raised his fist again. "You killed Celestina?"

"Damn right I did." Blood dripped from Ramon's nose. "I knew taking her away would hurt you in ways nothing else would."

Milan let him go, Ramon pushed him and the two intertwined, tussling on the floor.

"I'll kill you." Milan smashed his hand into Ramon's face, determining to break his nose. "How could you hurt Celestina?"

"Get off me!" Ramon yanked Milan's hair.

"Ah!" Milan punched him and crawled to the gun.

Ramon grunted, kicking it across the room.

"I don't need the gun!" Milan jumped on Ramon, strangling him. "I'll kill you with my bare hands."

"Get off!" Ramon grabbed his wrists. "Get the fuck off me."

George ran into the room and grabbed the gun from the floor. "Stop!"

Milan let Ramon go. "George?"

"Get off!" Ramon pushed Milan off, holding his red neck. "What the fuck you doing here, George?"

"Gray told me you were here."

"Well, good." Ramon got up, coughing. "You always pop in at the wrong time so this is a pleasant change." He spit blood by Milan's feet. "Anything to say, Milan?"

Milan stood, raising his eyebrows.

"You wanted to find George, right?" Ramon wiped blood from his nose. "Here he is."

Milan looked back and forth at them, his gaze settling on Ramon. "You knew where he was the whole time?"

Ramon tugged on his collar. "I was hiding him."

"Why?"

"He's my friend." Ramon's arrogance was still apparent despite the butt whipping Milan had given him. He hobbled to George and put his arm around his shoulders. "More of a friend than you ever were."

Milan laughed, gesturing to George. "You can't possibly believe he's your friend. He doesn't do anything that doesn't benefit himself."

The creases in George's forehead told Milan they were on the same page.

"I thought Anna made a fool of me," Milan said to Ramon. "But trusting you was the biggest mistake of my life."

Ramon's face glowed as if he found that a compliment. "George and Gray are my brothers and we're gonna split this lovely fortune once you're gone."

"Jesus." Milan shook his head, overwhelmed by enough secrets to last him a lifetime. "I should've listened to Douglas."

"Yeah, well you didn't." Ramon patted George's shoulder. "It's your lucky day huh, Georgie Boy. You got the gun. Might as well do the honors. Kill him."

"Look me in the eyes when you do it, George." Milan squinted as George's stare wavered and his hands shook. "I dare you."

"You heard me." Ramon pushed George in front of Milan. "Do it."

George raised his trembling arm.

"I'm not your enemy," Milan said. "I was after you because I thought you killed my father."

"Oh, what are we groveling now?" Ramon mocked. "Go on, George. Put him out of his misery."

"I never grovel." Authority laced Milan's voice to the point of even surprising him by his own strength. "If it's my time, it's my time but you look at both of us, George. Am I really the bad guy in this?"

"You're always the bad guy," Ramon said.

"George." Milan swallowed. "If you kill me then you do it knowing I treated you better than anyone ever did."

George's shoulders sunk.

"I always respected you. Never once tried to pull the wool over your eyes like this one." Milan pointed to Ramon who snickered in return. "You and I were always on the level. Even if we didn't agree, we knew where we stood."

"Oh, for Christ's sake." Ramon waved his arms. "Just shoot the bastard. This begging is laughable, Milan."

Milan stood back, accepting his fate.

"Kill him."

"Yeah, do it, George." Milan clasped his hands in front of him. "Shoot me."

George's shoulders vibrated as he looked away from Milan and then at him again.

"Do it," Ramon screamed.

"No." George turned the gun on Ramon. "I don't think so."

"What? I said pop this motherfucker. It's all we've wanted."

George's nostrils wiggled. "It's all *you've* wanted."

"Bullshit. Stop playing around and pop this fool."

"Sorry to burst your bubble, Ramon," George said. "I'm not the dumbass you think I am."

Ramon raised his chin. "What the fuck are you talking about?"

"It was you this whole time. You killed Luca and told Milan I did it."

"You need help, George." Ramon fidgeted, smacking his lips. "Mind going already? You ain't that old yet."

"Nothing's wrong with me but there is damn sure something wrong with you if you think I'm a fool."

"You better not even think of crossing me, George." Ramon pointed in his face. "After all I've done for you?"

"You haven't done shit but make empty promises. Talking about we'll be kings but you planned to sell me and Gray out from the beginning."

"Stop it." Ramon shook George. "Milan's getting in your head, man. None of this shit is true."

"I think for myself, and you're a bigger manipulator than Milan will ever be."

Milan smirked.

"You needed Gray and me to buy into your scheme." George raised the gun to Ramon's face. "Be a man and admit what a two-faced, backstabbing piece of shit you are."

Ramon snickered than laughed full out. "You better rethink what you're doing, George. I'll lead Vitale after tonight and your ass is grass if you betray me."

George squeezed the gun, exuding the confidence that Milan had always admired about him. "You ain't leading a damn thing."

Ramon moved his tongue around in his mouth. "Fuckin' nigger."

"There he goes!" Milan laughed, clapping. "The snake's shedding his skin. George meet the *real* Ramon."

"I know he's a snake." George squinted at Ramon, his trembles now seemed to be from anger instead of fear. "And who the fuck are you calling a nigger? Shit, I knew you probably did behind my back but now to my face, huh?"

"Milan's the enemy not me. I did this for my father."

"Bullshit," George said. "This was all because you wanted to prove something. You dishonored your father."

"You were more than willing to reap the rewards of Luca's death. So don't put this all on me."

"You didn't do this for your father." George panted. "You did it for greed. To get the money."

"No." Ramon raised an eyebrow. "That's the bonus."

Milan yanked Ramon and shook him. "He killed Celestina!"

"What?" George gasped.

"You son of a bitch. Pretending to share my grief," Milan yelled in Ramon's face. "Promising you'd help me avenge her death and it was you!"

"God," George whispered, grimacing. "Say this isn't true, Ramon."

"It was for the good of the business."

Milan shook him like a rag doll. "Good for business to kill the woman I loved?"

"Celestina was a distraction just like Anna is."

"She was a beautiful soul!" Milan shoved him. "She was everything good in the world."

"You're a sap. How a man of your caliber could let a woman wrap you around her finger is beyond me."

"That's love, asshole," Milan said. "Something you know nothing about."

"I loved my father and your dad took him away from me. Kill him, George."

"Fuck you."

"Fine." Ramon ran to the desk and got Milan's gun out the drawer. "I'll do it."

"Ramon," Milan roared.

"I'll take you both out." Ramon raised the gun. "I'm not the only one with a secret am I, George? Why don't you tell Milan what your daughter's been up to?"

George fidgeted.

"What?" Milan shook his hands out at George. "What is it now?"

"Anna Hampton doesn't exist," Ramon said. "She's Diana Wayans."

Milan's chest tightened. "What?"

"Yeah." Ramon staggered toward him. "Your precious, perfect little Anna is a lying slut."

"Shut up!" Milan rammed his head into Ramon's stomach, throwing him to the floor.

"Milan," George shouted.

He ripped the gun from Ramon and stood over him, aiming it at Ramon's face. "You said it's judgment day, right?"

"Fuck you." Ramon writhed on his back. "I don't regret a damn thing."

"Well, I guess we have more in common than I thought. Because I don't regret *this* either."

Ramon lifted his head, his eyes widening as Milan pulled the trigger.

Milan shot and the bullet ripped through Ramon's flesh.

Ramon gurgled blood, flopping and fidgeting until he no longer moved.

Milan dropped the gun on the carpet.

Even after knowing the truth, while looking at Ramon he still saw a man who was his closest friend dying in front of him.

"I'm sorry," George said.

Milan stared at the calm expression on Ramon's dead face. "I'm no better than he is."

"You have a heart," George said. "But this is the world you were born into so what can you do?"

Milan wiped Ramon's blood from his face. "You saved my life after I tried to take yours."

"I never would've hurt Luca. He was always kind to me like you were. I always looked past your lifestyle because I don't like people judging me either. You were always real with me, Milan.

That's all I can say."

"Is it true?" Milan looked at the blood splatter on his sleeves. "About Anna?"

"Yes."

"She has your eyes."

George smiled. "And my stubbornness."

"I was so taken with her I saw what I wanted to see." Milan snatched George's shirt. "You gotta help me."

George frowned. "What?"

"Tell her to come back to me. I don't care about what she did. I just want her back."

"I'm the last person she'd listen to about this." George removed Milan's hands from his shirt. "Whatever happens between you will be up to her."

"She's more amazing than I realized. She put her life on the line for you. You're a lucky man to have her as your daughter."

"Too bad I didn't realize it sooner. So it's all over?" George glanced at Ramon. "You won't hurt my daughter, right?"

"I'd kill myself before I hurt Anna." Milan batted his eyes, frantically. "I mean Diana." He pointed to Ramon. "What's his real name?"

"Lorenzo Bastiani. Federico's only child."

Milan closed his eyes, the revelations he'd learned consuming him. "Yep, I'm the biggest fool."

"How could you know? He was a damn good actor."

Milan jerked his eyes open. "So is your daughter."

George shrugged.

"Why did you save my life?"

"Because of Diana." George hooked his thumbs inside his belt loops. "She taught me if a man ain't decent then he ain't a man at all."

"Yeah." Milan half-smiled. "She taught me the same thing."

CHAPTER THIRTY-SIX

George's phone call left Diana even more confused as if that were possible. She mulled over it for a few moments and then knocked on the door which connected her and Eric's adjoining hotel rooms.

He walked into her room as she reclaimed her favorite spot by the window and looked at the ocean beaming under the magnificent moonlight.

"What is it?" Eric swept his hand across his drained face. "Please say you could get a flight for tomorrow because I'm sick as hell of this place."

"I got a flight." She opened the window, allowing the salty, aquatic air into the room. "It's at one p.m. so we need to be out of here by nine."

"Thank God." He plopped on the bouncy bed. "I never want to see Miami again."

She chuckled as various couples walked along the beach. "You used to like Miami."

"Is that all you wanted to tell me?" He stood, pointing back to his door while facing her. "I can go back to my room?"

"George just called me. Milan knows I'm Diana."

"What?"

"Ramon told him." She smiled, surprising herself. "It's okay. He won't hurt me or anything."

He squinted as he sat on the bed. "How can you be sure of that?"

She told Eric about Ramon trying to kill Milan and him thanking George for saving his life.

"Jesus." Eric paused as if he reflected over the story before asking, "Is George gonna be all right?"

"Milan gave him some money, and he's off to wherever again."

"That's it? You do all this for him and George just walks away? He can't even come to the hotel to say goodbye?"

She shrugged a shoulder, refusing to share another wasteful tear on her relationship with her father. "He promised he'll come see me in Atlanta, and I have to accept that's the best he can do."

Eric shook his head, frowning.

"You can't change people, Eric."

"No, but he should love you enough to *want* to change."

"George has been like this his whole life. I don't expect him to change now." She sat across from him on the bed, avoiding eye contact. "So, this mess is over."

"Uh, no it's not. There's a big elephant in the room, remember? The rich and powerful one who's been calling you all night."

She thought of Milan's pitiful voicemails begging her to talk to him. "It doesn't matter now."

"Milan's in love with you. He's not going to just walk away."

She pinched the loud, tropical bedspread. "You care about Milan now?"

"Hell no, but I know how he feels. You have a habit of breaking men's hearts and leaving them to repair the damage. You're..." He dropped his leg from the bed. "Never mind."

"No, say it."

"You take everything you can from a man and when you're done, you don't think about his feelings."

The words were some of the hardest to swallow because they were true.

"Look what you did to me, Diana. I let you control me because I was afraid of losing you. I'm not doing that anymore."

She looked at him, blinking.

"You've stepped all over my feelings and then I come here like a sap." He stabbed his index finger into the spread. "I put *my* life in danger for you, and you say you're grateful but is it just lip surface?"

She sighed.

"Shit, I don't even know if I'll have a job when I get back to Atlanta, but I'd do this again if it meant saving you." He stared at her, his bottom eyelids jumping. "Guess now I know why you risked your life for your father who doesn't do shit for you because I did the same thing." He went to the door. "I'll see you in the morning—"

"You're right."

He turned around.

"I've treated you horribly."

His eyebrows flattened.

"It took coming here and getting involved with Milan to admit what I've known since we broke up."

He inched to the bed. "What?"

"I'm also a fool." Her eyes watered. "Because I've been searching for something that's been right under my nose the entire time. It's you, Eric. Everything I've wanted and searched for is you."

He swayed, a deep scowl covering his forehead.

"I love you, Eric. I've always loved you and I know now I always will."

His bottom lip dropped.

"I'm so sorry for how I've treated you." She stroked the bedspread, closing her eyes. "Since I was a kid, I longed to have my father in my life. To have a man who would be there for me no matter what and I do. That's you, Eric. It's always been you."

He pinched his nose, sniffling.

"I'm sorry for knowing you were the best thing that ever happened to me and not grabbing you and never letting you go. I'm doing that now, Eric." She opened her eyes. "I can't let you go because you're a part of me, and I don't want to continue in this world without you."

He exhaled, his frown signaling confusion.

"Wasn't expecting that?" Diana snickered. "I wasn't intending to say it either. It just came out of me."

He formed a guarded smile. "Can more come out of you?"

She laughed, weeping. "I want another chance, Eric. If you can forgive me and let me love you, I promise you won't regret it."

"Is this real?" He sat beside her with wide eyes like a child who'd just met Santa Claus. "Please, tell me I'm not dreaming because my heart can't take it."

She grabbed him by his neck and pulled his lips into hers, feeling his heart pounding in his chest.

He whimpered as if she owned his heart and commanded it beyond his control.

Sticky, hot and wet, they played tag with each other's tongues. Each wanting to own the thrill the other felt.

She took her mouth away, sucking her lips to hold on to the kiss as long as possible. "I love you, Eric."

"I can't get hurt again, Di." He chewed his lip. "If we do this, we do it for the long haul. For the end of time."

She stroked his tensing bicep. "That's what I want."

"I mean it." He kissed her with both hands squeezing her face. "I want you forever. That means marriage and beyond."

She smiled, clamping her hands on his wrists. "Promise me forever."

He laid her flat on the bed, soaking her with domineering, wet kisses. "Forever." He got on top of her, gyrating his concrete frame against her hungry thighs.

Diana pushed her hands into his hair, moving his head back and forth as she sucked life out his kisses, knowing she'll never again have to remind herself how good it felt to be in the arms of the man she loved.

CHAPTER THIRTY-SEVEN

"Hello, Miss Wayans," Milan's butler greeted her and Eric at the security gate the next morning. "Mr. Vitale is waiting for you in the parlor. I'll escort you."

"No, that's okay." Diana's shaking hands got tangled in her purse strap. "I remember where it is."

The butler nodded and left.

Diana watched the bodyguard by the tree as she pulled Eric close. "I wish you hadn't made me come here."

"You gotta do this so we can move on." He wrapped his hands around hers. "Milan can't think he can be a part of your life. Be honest with him and end this."

"What do I say?" The breeze tickled her hair. "I lied to him."

"You don't owe Milan Vitale anything except closure."

A part of her would miss Milan's witty humor, lavish lifestyle and how he made her feel like the most desirable woman in the world, but she didn't love him.

"Di?" Eric lifted her chin. "You want closure too, right?"

"Yes." She covered his mouth in kisses. "I love you and only you."

"Mm." He caressed the curve in her back. "Then tell him."

"Okay." She took a deep breath, shaking away nerves. "What if he doesn't accept what I say?"

Eric let her go radiating with confidence as if he always knew he'd be the sole owner of Diana's heart. "Then that's on him."

Diana kissed him and rushed to the corridor as Douglas came out the mansion.

AFTER DIANA EXCHANGED greetings with Douglas and entered the mansion, Douglas sauntered toward Eric with a smile as if he'd made peace with something deep in his soul. "Detective Sachs." He gave Eric's hand a sturdy shake. "Didn't expect to see you here again."

"Diana needed to get things straight with Milan."

Douglas nodded, squinting from the sun.

"What are you doing here?"

The men started down the walkway that crossed the grass.

"Why wouldn't I be here?" Douglas moved with a nonchalant gait with his hands in his pockets. "I work here."

"I thought you were leaving."

"Weren't you the one who said I need to complete the mission?" He smiled. "Besides, the empire is still around and as long as it is, I will be. I'll make sure everyone associated with it pays for all they've done."

"But you've become close to Milan."

"I have, but I've never forgotten what he's capable of." Douglas wobbled his head. "Just because he's sparing Diana and her father doesn't mean he's changed. He's a product of what his father made him, a dangerous man, and he always will be."

"Maybe he really has changed." Eric couldn't believe the words coming out of his own mouth. "Trust me, Diana has that power."

"Thank you for being so nice to Pam." Douglas' elbow rubbed Eric's arm as they walked. "Other than me she didn't have many who cared about her."

"I can't believe she's gone. She was so full of life. I wish I'd known her longer."

"Milan's holding a memorial service for her." Douglas sucked his teeth, creases of anger filling his forehead. "She's dead because of his organization and now he's playing the martyr."

He stopped and held out his hand to Eric. "It was nice meeting you, Detective. If I'm ever in Atlanta, I'll look you up."

Eric smiled, shaking his hand. "Please do."

"And if you're ever back in Miami—"

"Ah." Eric grinned, waving his finger. "I don't plan on coming back here."

"Fair." Douglas patted Eric's shoulder and walked on. "If you change your mind, this is where I'll be."

DIANA FOUND MILAN WAITING for her outside the parlor.

He swayed with his hands in his pockets, eyes twitching.

They exchanged small smiles as she entered the room.

Milan eased the door closed and brushed up against her as he always did. "How are you?"

She took an anxious gulp. "I should ask you the same thing. You had a heck of a night I hear."

He exhaled as he nodded.

"Saw the cleaning crew in your office."

"They're trying to get the blood stains out." His gaze wandered away from her. "Part of me wants to keep them there as a memento."

She held her breath. "I hope that's a joke."

"I don't regret killing Ramon. He killed Celestina."

"I know." Diana patted his arm than stopped after noticing the yearning in his eyes. "I'm so sorry. Thank you for what you did for my father. Giving him money and everything."

"It was the right thing to do. Do you know where he's gone?"

"No."

"Same old George." Milan's nostrils widened when he chuckled. "Probably on a plane to Saskatchewan by now."

She laughed.

"God creates another heaven every time you smile."

She straightened her lips. "I'm so sorry about Celestina. Must be torture to realize the person who killed her was right here. Someone you loved and trusted."

"Celestina's death was my fault. I put her in a place where that monster could touch her, but it won't happen again." His eyes locked on her. "I won't allow anyone I love to be hurt anymore."

"I have to be at the airport." She glanced at her watch though she already knew the time. "Just wanted to say I'm sorry for what I did."

"What did you do?" He sat on the edge of the desk. "Seduce me and make me fall in love with you? You're not sorry, Anna. You'd do it again to save your father and you know what? It makes me want you even more."

"What?"

"You came here to say goodbye, but I won't accept that. You can tell yourself you felt nothing for me but it's not true."

"I came here because you deserve an apology and I need closure."

"But this isn't closure. You're pretending you don't want me."

"Stop it." She raised her palm to him. "I'm going back to Atlanta to live my life."

"This could be your life." He stood. "I don't care what you did. I love you and I know you love me too."

"Goodbye, Milan." She turned to leave and he gently grabbed her. "Let me go, please."

He stood close to her, sniffing her hair. "Give me a chance. You owe me that after playing with my heart."

"I don't owe you anything." She faced him. "You forget why I did this? You were trying to kill my father."

"Because I thought he killed *mine*." He moved back, standing on the rug between them. "Anna, we're the same person."

"No, we're not, and my name is Diana."

"Yes, we are. You did what you did for your father and I did what I did for mine and we'd both do it again."

"You hurt people." She squeezed her purse strap. "You murder and destroy lives."

"No more. You've made me a better a man."

"Milan, this is your *life*." She stood from the door. "The only life you've known and you can't change it."

"You mean the world to me, Anna."

"You fell in love with someone who wasn't real."

"You lifted me from the darkness and I fell for you." He shut his watering eyes. "I fell for you hard, Anna. Diana, whatever. I don't give a fuck about your name." He grabbed her again, squeezing. "I love the woman you are inside. Not the stuff you told me. I know you, Diana. More than any man ever could."

"What's my favorite color?"

He grimaced, relaxing his grip on her.

"It's not Anna's favorite color." She lifted her head. "What foods do I like to eat? I'll give you a hint, it's not what Anna likes to eat. All those art exhibits Anna went to overseas, I've never been out of the states in my life."

His face reddened.

"I said I was a social person, I'm not." She shrugged. "I'm an introvert and I love being at home."

He rubbed his knuckles. "Does humiliating me make you feel good because you're damn good at it."

"That's not my intention. Milan, I learned so much about myself while being with you, and I'm thankful because you opened my eyes to how fleeting love is."

"Exactly, Anna. We have to grab love when we find it because it's a gift we can't ever count on."

"I'm grabbing it." She chuckled as a tear fell. "I'm grabbing it with Eric because he's the man I want. I've never loved a man as much as I do him. We have history, and he's a part of me."

"You're a part of *me*." He touched her cheek, and she closed her eyes knowing the smell of his cologne would forever be in her memory. "Eric's the past. Let me be the future."

"No."

"I promise to give you the life you've dreamed of. It starts right here." He spread his arms wide. "Pick a room in the house."

"What?"

"Any room and it will be your space for your graphic design business. Better yet, I'll buy you a building of your own to work from."

"Milan—"

"No, listen." He rubbed his hands, awkwardly. "You'll have a design empire when we're through. I'll invest in it and you can have a staff and crew. I'll get you the most influential clients in the world and you'll be the biggest thing before you know it."

"Milan."

He took her hand. "I'm offering you the opportunity of a lifetime, Anna. Anything you want or need I will give you."

"Can you give me Eric? If not, there's nothing else I want."

"Stop it." He wrapped his arms around her, forcing his damp lips on hers as she turned from his kisses. "Stop lying." He held her head still so he could kiss her.

"You want me. I'm gonna make you prove it."

"Mm, no." She tightened her lips, pushing at him. "Milan, please. Don't do this."

"I love you." He panted among the harsh kisses. "You want me. I can feel it. I always felt it."

"No." She pushed at his chest, turning her head left and right as he kissed her so hard she couldn't breathe. "No," she mumbled and groaned. "Don't do this."

"Don't leave me." He pressed his forehead against hers, squeezing her waist. "I love you so damn much. I need you."

"No!" She pushed him away. "It's over."

"I'm not letting you leave here until you admit it." He wiped her lipstick from his mouth. "Admit you fell for me."

She shook her head. "No."

"You can't fake how you shiver whenever I touch you or how hot your skin gets when I kiss you. You love me," he growled. "Say it."

She didn't and after a moment he slinked to his desk with his head low.

"When I came here," Diana spoke. "I didn't give a damn about how this would affect you but it crushes me how I've hurt you."

He slumped in the chair.

"Milan, you told me you want people to see the real you. I did." She touched her chest, sniffling. "You can have comfort knowing that I saw the real man underneath all this other shit and I liked him. I liked him a lot."

"Bet you and Eric had a good laugh at my expense, didn't you?" His nostrils flared. "What? Would you come over here whispering sweet words in my ear then go back to the hotel and make love to him?"

"No."

STACY-DEANNE

"Don't lie." He pointed at her. "Every night you laid in his arms, laughing at the game you played so brilliantly."

"*No*. It wasn't like that."

"What the fuck am I supposed to do?" He punched the desk, sobbing. "Just let you walk out of my life? Forget you ever existed? You're a horrible person, Diana. You stole my heart and didn't give a damn about me."

She approached the desk, holding out her hand. "That's not true."

"You studied me like a book and came in here with your sweet smile, beautiful eyes and lies!" His face tore with despair. "Every moment we shared, every kiss we had, was a lie!"

She went to speak but just shook her head.

"Don't give me that shit about wanting closure." He dug his nails into the desk. "You came here to set your conscience straight because in your warped head you want me to forgive you, well go fuck yourself, Diana.

As long as I live I'll never, ever forgive you for this."

She looked at the carpet, shoulders trembling.

"All my time and money I spent wasted on lies and deceit and there's one thing you didn't even realize, Anna."

She looked at him.

"You didn't realize..." He released a tiny breath between his words. "That I love you so much you didn't have to sneak around about being George's daughter. I'd have told you anything you wanted because I was so gone over you it wouldn't have mattered."

She covered her mouth, sobbing.

"So don't tell me I don't love you and what I felt wasn't real." He sat back, stroking the desk. "You breaking my heart is payback for the things I've done. I get it. I'll do my best to never fall in love again."

"Don't say that, please."

"I'm destined to be alone forever. God used you as a tool to teach me a lesson and it's one I won't ever forget. So fuck it, right?" He smiled, wincing. "Might as well go back to the Milan everyone expects. Continue leading the empire."

"You are better than this life, Milan. You've done horrible things but you can change."

"I was *trying* to change." He clasped his hands, chuckling with sarcasm. "*You* were my reason for changing and look how that's turned out. I'm alone again with my notebook and you'll be with Eric. That's what you want? You're giving up all of this for a cop who probably uses all-you-can-eat coupons when he takes you out to dinner?"

"Don't make fun of Eric and yes he's what I want." She stood straight. "For love, I'd give up anything. You would too."

"I did with you, but I never will again."

"I wish you knew how badly I feel about this."

He clapped, breathing hard through his nostrils. "You need an Academy Award, Miss Wayans."

"Milan—"

"Now if you don't mind, get the fuck out my house and never come back." His glare dug into her soul. "I never want to see you again."

She sighed, her hand shaking as she took the necklace he'd given her from her purse. "I'm sorry, Milan." She laid it in front of him as he closed his eyes. "I really am."

She gave him one last look as she walked to the door and left.

THE END

To receive book announcements subscribe to Stacy's mailing list: Mailing List[1]

---

1. http://eepurl.com/dFGzTL

Also by Stacy-Deanne

Standalone